DANNY ORLIS

AND

DEEDEE'S BEST FRIEND

DANNY ORLIS

AND

DEEDEE'S BEST FRIEND

BERNARD PALMER

Please note that several books in the Danny Orlis series are published by Sword of the Lord Publications and are available for purchase on their website, www.swordbooks.com.

Aneko Press *Youth*

www.anekopress.com

Aneko Press, Life Sentence Publishing, and our logos are trademarks of Life Sentence Publishing, Inc.
203 E. Birch Street
P.O. Box 652
Abbotsford, WI 54405

JUVENILE FICTION / Religious / Christian / Action & Adventure

Paperback ISBN: 979-8-88936-056-8

eBook ISBN: 979-8-88936-057-5

10 9 8 7 6 5 4 3 2 1

Available where books are sold

CONTENTS

Ch. 1: DeeDee's New Friend 1

Ch. 2: Kent's Best Christmas 11

Ch. 3: Overnight Visit 19

Ch. 4: Cutest Fellow in School 29

Ch. 5: Indian Friend 41

Ch. 6: Doug's New Appearance 53

Ch. 7: DeeDee's Admirer 67

Ch. 8: Unwanted Invitation 77

Ch. 9: Solved Problem 87

Ch. 10: Secret Party 97

Ch. 11: Guilt Feelings 113

CHAPTER 1

DEEDEE'S NEW FRIEND

It was early in the afternoon at Fairview Junior High. Decorations draped the windows and a Christmas tree filled one corner of the room. A festive air had taken on the class and even the teacher, who was known for her unsmiling discipline and mountainous homework, was gay and somewhat tolerant and understanding.

But DeeDee Davis was unaffected by the mood. She glanced uneasily out the window once more, noting that clouds now hid the sun and snow was spitting against the window to her right. If this kept up, they wouldn't be able to go the next day when school was out, and that would ruin everything.

Sandra Cole, who was sitting in front of DeeDee, squirmed around and smiled. DeeDee's breath caught in her throat, and she risked a quick smile in response.

"Let's have lunch together," Sandy said, forming the words soundlessly with her mouth.

DeeDee nodded, weak and trembling inside. This was all a dream! It couldn't be happening! Sandy Cole wouldn't want to make friends with her! Not someone as popular as Sandy. DeeDee felt twin spots of color spread across her cheeks.

She had known who Sandy was the first week she and the boys came to school. Everybody in junior high knew Sandy Cole. The vivacious, blue-eyed blonde was one of the class officers, a cheerleader and soprano in the girls' quartet. She was the most "in" girl in their class. Everybody wanted to run with her.

And her clothes! DeeDee had scarcely been able to believe that Sandy actually owned all the different outfits she wore. It seemed that she never wore the same dress twice; at least not twice in the same week. And every outfit looked as though it had been especially designed for her. Even her shoes were striking.

Actually, it had been Sandy's clothes that caused DeeDee to get acquainted with her in the first place. Sandy came to school one morning wearing such a stunning outfit that DeeDee could not contain herself.

"That's a beautiful dress, Sandy," she exclaimed.

The other girl's smile flashed.

"Why, thank you, DeeDee. I'm so glad you like it."

"It matches the blue of your eyes exactly."

Sandy beamed. And, after that, she always had a smile and a word or two for DeeDee. But DeeDee had never supposed their friendship would ever go any farther than that. Sandy wasn't the kind of a girl to choose someone like her. Not that Sandy was wild or anything like that. She was just different. She lived in one of the biggest and newest homes in Fairview, for one thing. And her folks had two new cars and took trips to places like Bermuda and Las Vegas. Sandy was always talking about some exciting place they had just visited.

DeeDee would have liked to have gotten better acquainted with Sandy, but she knew it would never happen.

At least she had *thought* it would never happen. Now, Sandy had asked her to eat lunch with her! Suddenly the gloom vanished and DeeDee was so excited that she waited impatiently for noon to come.

Sandra was waiting for her in the corridor when their last class of the morning was over.

"Hi, DeeDee." Sandy's smile was more warm and inviting than ever. "You didn't have anybody to eat lunch with today, did you?"

DeeDee hesitated. She had half promised one of the girls from church, but she could eat with her anytime.

"No," she said aloud. "I didn't promise anyone I'd eat with them today."

Sandy smiled and touched her arm. "I'm glad. I've been wanting to get better acquainted with you."

They went down to the lunchroom together. DeeDee

imagined that half the girls in her class were eyeing her enviously. She knew what they were thinking because she had thought the same thing herself when she had seen others in the favored position of being with Sandy. She couldn't get over the fact that Sandy had been the one who had sought her out – that she had picked her from among all the other girls in their class. At least she hoped she had picked her. A brief spasm of fear seized her. Maybe the other girl was just feeling sorry for her. Maybe they would eat together once and that would be the end of it. If that happened, she would just die!

"What are you going to do for Christmas?" Sandy asked when they were seated and had started to eat.

"We're going to the School for the Blind," DeeDee explained. For an instant she was half ashamed of the fact that they were going to a place like that to spend Christmas with Kent and Jill Gilbert. But Sandy seemed most interested.

"How exciting! We're going to Minneapolis and have dinner in one of the big hotels." She wrinkled her nose distastefully. "I get so tired of it I could scream."

"Tired of it?" DeeDee echoed, eyes widening. "You can't be serious. It sounds super to me."

"You wouldn't think so if you'd done it for the past four or five years." A certain wistfulness crept into her voice. "I'd give anything to be able to stay at home for just *one* Christmas – or at least be with our whole family. But Dad can't have it that way.

He's got to be at a hotel or a supper club where–"
She stopped, as though suddenly realizing that she
was saying things she shouldn't.

DeeDee couldn't help staring at her new friend.
She had supposed that *all* families got together at
Christmas time. She had never imagined there were
those who didn't. Going to a big hotel dining room
would be fun, she had to admit, but she wouldn't
want to do it on Christmas at the expense of being
with the rest of the Orlis family. She didn't blame
Sandy for not liking it.

Finally, they finished eating lunch and went back
to their homeroom. DeeDee had difficulty in keeping her mind on her studying. Even the snowfall
that was increasing steadily, failed to dim the gaiety
that sparkled in her eyes. Sandy Cole liked her. She
actually liked her!

* * *

The day before Christmas was strangely quiet at the
Minnesota School for the Blind. Classes had been
dismissed two days before and most of the students
and faculty had gone to their homes for the holidays.
Even the superintendent and his family had gone to
visit relatives, leaving Kent and Jill Gilbert with Miss
Tyler, an older teacher who had volunteered to stay
with them. There was a Christmas tree in the lounge
where Kent and Jill were sitting, but nobody had

bothered to turn on the lights. The usually bustling room was empty except for the two of them.

Kent shuffled slowly across the carpeted floor to an easy chair in front of the fireplace. Groping behind him for the arms of the recliner, he dropped into it heavily and pushed himself back into a more comfortable position.

"Some Christmas this is going to be." Disappointment edged his voice. "I don't suppose we'll even get a Christmas dinner."

"I–I'm sorry, Kent," Jill said, her voice reflecting her brother's gloom. "I'm sorry I got sick so we couldn't go to Fairview."

Kent sat upright. "It's not your fault," he told her quickly. "And this isn't going to be such a bad Christmas. In fact, it's going to be a great Christmas – for just the two of us."

"You're just saying that." But she had to admit it did make her feel better hearing Kent talk that way, even though she knew he didn't really mean it. She turned for a time and stared out the window. It hadn't been snowing hard, but for the past few days the weather had been threatening. Even now, new flakes were drifting silently down to lay a fresh white sheen on the drifts of former storms.

"It was nice to have Christmas with Danny and Kay, wasn't it?" Kent said, at last.

"I think it was the very best day of the whole year.

Everybody was at the house laughing and talking at the same time."

"And Danny would read the Christmas story."

"And Kay would lead us in a few Christmas carols," Jill added.

They sat there for a while, remembering.

"Old Jim ought to be home from CBI," Kent said. "I sure would like to be there and hear him tell about all the fun the guys have in the dorm."

"I'm sure Uncle Carl and Aunt Mary will be down from the Angle," Jill went on, "and maybe Ron and Darlene will be there."

"Yeah." Kent smiled. "I'd like to be there just to see that little guy of theirs."

It used to bother Jill when her brother spoke about "seeing" somebody or something because he was blind. Then she had realized that he meant almost the same as she did when she used the word. He only "saw" in a different way. His other senses took the place of his eyes.

"He must be about six months old, I guess," Kent went on, breathing deeply. He had never paid much attention to how old anybody's babies were, but this one was special, at least to him. Ron and Darlene had named the little guy after him. John Kent Orlis. Kent had tried to pretend that hadn't pleased him particularly. He couldn't have the other guys at school knowing how he felt about it; they might tease him, if they did. But he had been pleased about it – more pleased than he would ever admit to anyone. And the thing that meant the most to him was Ron's reason for naming his son after him. He had written it to Kent and Jill in the letter telling them about the birth of their son.

"We decided on that name, Kent," Ron had explained, "because we would like for him to have the same love for the Lord Jesus Christ that you have."

"Isn't that nice?" Jill exclaimed when she read it.

Kent scowled. "Isn't what nice?"

"Naming their baby after you." Her eyes shone. "It makes me proud of you, Kent."

"Well," he grumbled, "just see that you don't go blabbing it all over. What's in that letter isn't anyone else's business."

They had never talked about it again except when they pooled their savings from their allowances and bought a gift for little John Kent. Jill had picked it out and wrapped it after taking it home and showing it to her brother. Jill thought about all that as she sat quite still in the lounge. She pulled her robe closer about her and stared at the floor. If she hadn't gotten sick, they could have gone to Fairview for Christmas. They wouldn't be stuck here at the school. She was feeling better now, but it was too late. There wasn't time for them to go to Fairview now, and besides, they didn't have a way.

"This is going to be the worst Christmas we ever had," she muttered, feeling very sorry for herself.

Kent did not answer her. He was hunched forward, hands working nervously. He straightened suddenly.

"Did you hear that?"

Jill listened, but she couldn't hear anything. Still, she was sure there was something outside that had caught her brother's attention. That had often happened since Kent had been blind. She didn't know whether he was just listening better, or whether God had sharpened his hearing to make up for his blindness; but it was true that his ears caught things nobody else heard.

"What was it?" she asked uneasily.

"A car just drove into the yard."

"Are you sure?" she asked. But she showed that she believed him by getting to her feet and starting toward the window.

"They're getting out now," Kent continued. "The car door slammed."

"I wonder who–" Jill began. The words choked in her throat as she recognized the people who were approaching the front door.

"Who is it?" Kent demanded.

"It's Danny and Kay and the triplets!"

The corners of Kent's mouth twitched convulsively. He didn't say anything, but for an instant he was afraid he was going to cry. And that would never do; he couldn't have them see him blubbering.

"And Kent!" his sister blurted, her excitement growing with each passing second. "They've got packages and everything!"

"They must have come to spend Christmas with us," he mumbled. "Imagine that!"

As he spoke, he moved to Jill's side. Even as he did so he heard two more cars drive in and come to a stop.

"There's Uncle Carl and Aunt Mary!" Jill told him, the words tumbling out, one upon the other. "And there's Jim Morgan and some girl I've never seen before – and Ron and Darlene and their baby!"

She ran to the door to meet them. Kent was only half a pace behind.

For a time, all was confusion. Jim introduced Connie to Kent and Jill, and the Gilbert kids got acquainted with the newest member of the Orlis household, Ron and Darlene's baby. For a while everybody was laughing and talking at once. That was the situation when Miss Tyler came in. Jill stopped what she was doing long enough to introduce the matron to the rest of the family.

"I'm so glad you were able to come," Miss Tyler said. "Jill and Kent have been feeling a little bit discouraged at the thought of having to spend Christmas here alone."

Kay turned to her. "When I called to make arrangements about coming, the person who answered the phone said the kitchen help would be gone for the day but that we could do our own cooking, if we wished."

The matron nodded. "Would you like to go to the kitchen now?"

CHAPTER 2

KENT'S BEST CHRISTMAS

Kent was still standing in the middle of the floor, his face beaming, when another car drove up.

"There's somebody else out there," he said.

At first Jill didn't hear him. She was too busy playing with the baby.

"Jill," he said, raising his voice. "There's some more company out there for somebody. I just heard a car." She gave the baby back to Darlene and turned to the window.

"Oh!" A thin gasp escaped her lips.

"Who is it?" Kent's voice grew harsh. "Who's there?" His sister tried to answer him, but she could not. The words would not come.

"Who is it?" he demanded again. "Answer me!"

"It–it's Mother and Dad!"

Kent sucked in a quick breath. Mother and Dad! It couldn't be! They hadn't been to see them for at least three years – not since the authorities had taken him and Jill away from them. They hadn't even been interested enough in where they were or who they were living with to write or come and visit them. In fact, they hadn't even appeared at the trial when the judge made his decision to remove him and Jill from their home. Kent had the idea that they had been glad to get rid of them.

Now they had come to see them and he didn't even know if–if they knew about his eyes.

But they did. He could tell by the strangled whimper of pity that escaped his mother's lips when she saw him.

"Oh, Kent!" She started to sob. "Kent, I didn't know. Until last week I didn't know that you–you can't see anymore."

He comforted her as best he could. "That's OK, Mom," he said. "I'm going to make out all right. When I graduate from high school here, I'm going on to college. I'll manage real well."

For a time, she cried uncontrollably while Kent tried to talk to her. But gradually she gained control of herself enough to talk without crying. Then she turned her attention to her daughter.

Mr. Gilbert took Kent's hand and shook it vigorously. There were tears in his voice, if not in his eyes.

"Mother and I have been doing a lot of serious thinking lately," he said, "about the fact that we–we didn't provide a good home for you."

"Aunt Ethel lost both of her children in a fire Thanksgiving Day," their mother broke in. "That woke us up to what we had done to you. We started to look for you."

"At first no one would tell us anything," Mr. Gilbert continued, "but finally we were able to trace you to the welfare office in Fairview. Mr. Collins told us about your–your accident so we made arrangements to come over here and spend Christmas with you."

Kay and Mary Orlis had fixed most of the Christmas dinner at home, so it didn't take long for them to reheat the turkey and cook the vegetables. While that was going on everyone else was sitting in a big circle, asking questions and talking endlessly.

Kent leaned back and listened. He could place each voice, each tone, and characteristic phrase. There was Uncle Carl whose voice was deep and gruff. He remembered how afraid of him he had been at first, until he learned that was only the older man's manner. Then there was his own dad's bitter whine, and the bite to his mother's words. Each voice brought memories rushing back.

Some of those things were hard to think upon. It hurt too much to call them to mind. They made him think of those weeks and months when he and Jill had first gone to Fairview to live with Danny and Kay and how rebellious he had been. They made him think of the times when he had turned his back on the Lord, fighting desperately against the longing in his heart to confess his sin and take a stand for Christ. If he had done that the first time he wanted to, he knew he would probably not be blind. But he hadn't; he had determined to live his own life and this was the result.

Now dinner was almost ready. Danny gathered the group around a long table in the dining room. Mr. and Mrs. Gilbert wanted to go to a nearby café for dinner, but the others pressed them to stay.

"And besides," Danny said, "you're going to want to spend as much time as possible with Kent and Jill."

"But this is a family affair," Mr. Gilbert said. "We wouldn't think of breaking in."

Danny's smile said more than his words. "In our family, there's always room for more."

And so, reluctantly, the Gilberts stayed.

Before starting to serve, Kay called upon Carl Orlis. "Dad, we would like to have you take charge of our little program before we start to eat."

Carl nodded. "When you asked me about it yesterday," he began, "I got my Bible and turned to the second chapter of Luke. I planned to read the Christmas story, as we usually do on Christmas Day. But I've decided to do something different this time. I thought it might be interesting and helpful to us if we would have a short time of testimony." He paused, looking about quietly. "Is there anyone who would like to tell us what Christmas means to him?"

Usually at such meetings there was a short wait

before anyone spoke, but the instant Carl finished, Kent pushed back his chair and stood.

"Christmas means everything to me," he began. "If it wasn't for Christmas, we wouldn't have a Savior. I–I would still be like I was when I lived at home."

His dad scooted back in his chair and coughed nervously.

"I might even be in a reform school or something like that," Kent continued. "Now I'm here in school learning and having a lot of fun. And I'm not afraid of anybody because I'm not breaking the law. I no longer do a lot of things I'm not supposed to." For half a minute he hesitated, fumbling for words. "Christmas means Jesus Christ and happiness to me," he concluded awkwardly.

There was a taut silence. This was something that had been totally unexpected. Even Carl had not thought Kent would speak up or say what he did.

Danny, who happened to be looking at Mr. Gilbert when his son finished, saw the color drain from the man's cheeks, leaving them ashen. Before anyone else had time to get to his feet or begin to talk, Mr. Gilbert brought his hands down on the table, palms downward, with a resounding slap that rattled the plates and silver. In another sudden movement he jumped to his feet.

"Get our coats, Irma!" he snarled. "We're getting out of here!"

She stared at him as though he had suddenly gone out of his mind.

"But we haven't eaten yet," she protested.

"Don't you think I know it?"

"Then why don't you wait until we've had dinner, at least," she said. "It isn't polite to leave this way, just before the meal is to be served."

"If you want to stay, go ahead and stay!" he exclaimed bitterly. "I'll be at the hotel when you're ready to come!"

With that he stormed into the bedroom, slammed his hat on his head and marched out, still struggling into his topcoat.

For a full minute nobody spoke. A cloud descended over the little group, blotting out the last trace of merriment . At last Mrs. Gilbert found words.

"I–I'm sorry about Charles," she apologized. "He–he doesn't have much use for religion."

Kent got to his feet at that moment and turned in the direction of the door. Danny followed him.

"Where are you going, Kent?" he asked.

"Dad didn't open the outside door," the blind boy said. "He only went as far as the top of the stairs."

"That's interesting."

"I thought I'd go up and–and see if I could talk to him."

"I'll go with you."

They found Charles Gilbert standing before the outside door, his overcoat still unbuttoned, staring out over the bleak snow-covered grounds. He turned to stare at Danny, misery gleaming in his eyes.

"I'm sorry I exploded that way in there a minute ago. I just couldn't take it any longer, that's all."

"I understand," Danny told him.

"I'm not mad at anybody, Orlis," he continued, "but it sort of shakes a guy up to hear his own kid talk that way." He tried desperately to excuse himself. "I haven't been so bad. Since they took Kent and Jill away from us, I've quit drinkin' and have held down a good job. And we were beginning to think we could get them back, maybe–" His voice choked.

"I'm glad to hear that, Mr. Gilbert." Danny smiled warmly. "Why don't you come in and sit down for a few minutes. There are some things I'd like to talk over with you."

Once they were seated in the far corner of the lounge, Danny explained the way of salvation, using Bible verses to show that nobody can live the sort of life God wants him to live in his own strength. Danny was only dimly aware that Kent had left them. He supposed the boy was a little embarrassed at some of the things he was saying. That often happened with Christians who were older and more experienced in the things of God than the blind boy. However, Kent came back a few moments later with his mother. The four of them sat together, going over God's plan for saving the souls of men and women.

"I've got to admit that it sounds good," Mr. Gilbert

said, "but I don't know whether I could put much stock in it or not. The church has so many hypocrites in it."

"Unfortunately, that's true," Danny said. "Every organization or group, whether it's Christian or not, has a lot of hypocrites in it. That's because man is sinful by nature. But right now, we're not talking about the church or any other group of people. We're talking about a personal relationship with the Lord Jesus Christ. This is what each church member has to have to get to heaven. This is what *you* have to have to get to heaven."

That explanation seemed to satisfy Gilbert's objection of hypocrites in the church, but he had other questions. Many of them. Both he and his wife fired them at Danny. The youthful missionary answered each one with a reference from the Bible.

Finally, Mr. Gilbert nodded. "That's what's wrong with my life," he said seriously.

A moment later both of them knelt to pray, asking God's forgiveness through the blood of the Lord Jesus Christ.

Kent's heart began to sing. Suddenly he realized that he had to get down to tell Jill what had happened. This wasn't their worst Christmas! It was the best one they had ever had!

CHAPTER 3

OVERNIGHT VISIT

The week after Christmas vacation at Fairview Junior High, DeeDee stayed all night with her new friend, Sandra Cole. Sandy had asked her earlier in the week, but she hadn't been able to tell her whether she could or not until after she talked with Kay. And when she did talk with Kay she had to wait until she talked it over with Danny.

That was just one of the bad things about having to live with people as straitlaced and "religious" as Danny and Kay, she told herself. Sandy got to do whatever she wanted to, and she didn't have to ask anyone. She said her mother didn't care who she was with, or where she went, or anything. But Kay had to know all about what she planned to do, where she was going, and who she was with. And, as if that wasn't enough, she always insisted that she be in on time too.

But there wasn't anything DeeDee could do about it. She had to wait until they made up their minds. She was afraid they wouldn't let her go over to the Cole home to stay overnight, and she would just die if they didn't.

But finally, Kay had decided that it would be all right, so she was spending the night in one of the biggest and most beautiful homes in Fairview. She smiled inwardly, hoping her excitement didn't show. She was going to be staying with Sandy because the other girl liked her. She actually liked her and wanted her as a friend!

Since DeeDee's brother Doug had starred in the last basketball game, that was just about all Sandy wanted to talk about. She raved about the way he stood – how cute he was – his graceful movements when he dribbled down the court, and a lot of other things that DeeDee thought were ridiculous.

She couldn't understand what Sandy was raving about. Doug was just her brother who teased her most of the time and didn't want to go places with her or do anything with her. Although she didn't say anything, she wondered if there was something wrong with Sandy that kept her from seeing Doug as he really was. He sure wasn't all that great.

After dinner that evening Mr. and Mrs. Cole went out somewhere, leaving the two girls alone. Sandy didn't like it much, but DeeDee thought it was exciting. They watched television for a while before going up to Sandy's room. DeeDee looked about enviously as they moved from room to room. The big house was something of a dream to her.

But it was Sandy's room that staggered her. She stood in the doorway, staring about in admiration. She had never even known there could be rooms like this one, let alone for a girl her age. It was too wonderful to be true.

Sandy saw her reaction and allowed herself a faint smile. "Like it?" she asked.

"Like it?" DeeDee echoed. "It–it's–." There were no words for her to express what she thought of the room. The carpet was a beautiful shade of blue, making a perfect background for the ivory bedroom furniture. The wallpaper looked like some sort of cloth, only it wasn't, and the pictures could have come from the exclusive interior decorator's place in Minneapolis that DeeDee and Kay had gone by one day. They were that strikingly beautiful.

And a bathroom of her very own! It was no wonder that Sandy always looked so nice. She could fix her hair without having someone yelling at her to get out of the bathroom so he could wash or brush his teeth before the bus came.

"It's beautiful!" DeeDee exclaimed in a soft whisper.

DeeDee hesitated for an instant. But when Sandy didn't ask her to take a chair, she entered the room timidly and sat down at the dressing table. Sandy crossed to an easy chair and sat down.

"This room's all right, I guess," she said. "I really wanted the bedroom at the head of the stairs, but Daddy and Mother had already chosen it. So, I had to settle for this, even though it isn't as nice as the bigger one."

She leaned back and surveyed the room herself, as though she was actually seeing it for the first time.

"It's getting sort of tacky now," she said, "but I've been working on Mother. I think she's going to have it redecorated in the spring."

"Redecorated?" Awe crept back into DeeDee's voice, "I wouldn't change a thing!"

Sandy shrugged. "You wouldn't think that if you had to live in it for a while. I'm so tired of it I could scream."

With that she went over and turned on the MP3 player. DeeDee hadn't spent much time listening to the sort of songs Sandy had. Danny and Kay frowned on them, for one thing, and she hadn't thought she enjoyed them herself. Now, however, with Sandy sitting entranced, eyes closed, and keeping time to the music with her hands, DeeDee tried to like them.

After a while Sandy grew tired of the MP3 player and switched it off.

"Let's go down to the kitchen and see if we can find something to eat," she said. She opened her large closet and took out two housecoats. "Here, put this on."

DeeDee scarcely heard her. She was staring at the

clothes in the big closet and the row of shoes on the floor beneath them. DeeDee had never seen so many different dresses and shoes outside of a store. And nothing looked as though it had ever been worn.

"What beautiful clothes!"

"These?" Sandy echoed. "There isn't a decent thing in here. I just hate every one of them. Mother and I are going to Minneapolis one of these days and get me some new things."

DeeDee reached out mechanically and fingered the material in one of the dresses. It was just like being in a dress shop. A strange, wistful look came into her eyes.

* * *

DeeDee thought she had never had such a good time in her life as she had at Sandra's house that night. They listened to the radio, talked until almost two o'clock, and slept until almost noon the next day. DeeDee spent a leisurely hour in Sandy's bathroom taking a shower and fixing her hair.

"You don't know how lucky you are having a bathroom all your own."

Sandy stared at her. "Don't you?"

"We have one bathroom for five of us. I can hardly ever be in there as long as I want without someone screaming that I've been taking all day. This is wonderful!"

Sandy eyed her pathetically. "I don't see how you can stand it," she said. "I honestly don't."

Some of the bloom went out of DeeDee's excitement and happiness. It really wasn't easy to live with Danny and Kay and not have a bathroom of her own, a nice big bedroom with gorgeous furniture, and all the clothes she wanted. But the instant the thought came, DeeDee fought it down. Still, it was some time before she could laugh and enjoy herself again.

In the middle of the afternoon DeeDee asked about using the phone so she could call Kay to come for her. However, when she went to the kitchen to phone, Mrs. Cole volunteered to drive her out to the Orlis home.

"I don't like to trouble you," she said uneasily.

"It won't be any trouble at all. We've got some shopping to do anyway."

"But we live out in the country a couple of miles or so."

"That's perfectly all right. I'm so glad to have had you stay with Sandy." For an instant, the smile left her lips. "I'm glad to have her associate with nice girls."

Sandy came in just then and Mrs. Cole changed the subject quickly.

DeeDee rode home in the Cole car. She got out at the gate, thanked Sandy and her mother once more and went into the house.

Kay looked up. "Oh, it's you, DeeDee," she said. "I didn't hear you come in."

"I was going to call you, but Mrs. Cole and Sandy had to do some shopping, so they brought me home." Her face was still flushed with excitement.

"I wish you had asked them in. I would like to have met them."

The girl's smile faded. She looked uneasily about the Orlis home. She had always been proud of it before. She had thought it so cheery – even though the living room furniture was beginning to show definite signs of wear. She had liked nothing more on a cold winter day than to sit before the fireplace eating popcorn and listening while Danny read from the Bible or told some of his flying experiences. Now, she thought guiltily, she saw the place as it really was – faded and cheap and a little old-fashioned.

"Mrs. Cole was in a big hurry," the girl explained. "She couldn't have come in."

DeeDee didn't say it, but she was glad they hadn't come in. How could she ever invite them into a place such as this when they lived in such a beautiful home themselves? She just couldn't have done it.

She took her suitcase into her own bedroom and set it down. For the first time the room seemed drab and unattractive to her. She noticed that the wallpaper was faded and needed to be replaced. And the furniture! She shuddered. She didn't know why she had always thought her furniture was so nice, when actually it wasn't. Sandy would rather sleep on the floor than have a bed like hers.

DeeDee stood in the center of the room, turning slowly to view it with a critical eye. She just might be able to talk Danny into redoing her room before long; he had said something about it once several months ago. But even as she considered that prospect – as remote as it was – she realized that painting and papering wouldn't make it nice – not nice like Sandy's room.

DeeDee opened her suitcase and began to take out her clothes and put them in the closet. It was strange that she had never noticed before, but the clothes Danny and Kay bought for her were really cheap. Oh, they looked nice enough, she had to admit, or had looked nice when they were new. But the material was nothing like that in Sandy's clothes, and she had to wear what she got for ages and ages.

How could she ever hope to keep a girl like Sandy for a friend when she didn't have any nice clothes to wear? DeeDee pulled in a thin breath and expelled the air slowly. She felt guilty for even thinking it, but she suddenly realized that she was ashamed of Danny and Kay.

* * *

However, in spite of DeeDee's feelings of inferiority, the night she spent at Sandy's was the beginning of a warm friendship. The two girls got together in the hall for a few minutes before class in the morning, and they always ate together at noon. And when the basketball games were played, it was only natural that they would go together.

"I'll have to be leading cheers," Sandy said, "but that'll only be part of the time, so I could come and sit with you, DeeDee." Her smile winked invitingly. "That is, if you would like to save me a seat."

"If I'd like to?" DeeDee could not keep the awe and admiration from her voice.

They were a little late getting down to the gym for the next game. Doug Davis was already suited up and on the floor when they came in.

"There's your brother," Sandy told her.

DeeDee nodded. She didn't know what was so wonderful about that. She saw him every day, and sometimes she saw him a lot more than she wanted to when he was in one of those teasing, critical moods of his.

"Aren't you going to wave to him?"

DeeDee eyed her curiously. "Wave to him?" she echoed. "Why would I want to wave to Doug?"

"So he'll know you're here."

DeeDee snorted at the suggestion. "He knows I'm here, all right. We were talking about it this morning and I told him I was coming."

Sandy pouted. "If I had a brother who was playing basketball, I'd wave to him," she said. "I'd let him know that I'd come out to the game to support him."

That suggestion of Sandy's was just about the silliest

DeeDee had ever heard; but if Sandy wanted her to wave to Doug, she guessed she could. Self-consciously she stood and waved a small hand. Sandy joined her.

"Doug!" her friend called out. "Hi, Doug!"

On the basketball court, Doug heard his name and glanced up. DeeDee! he thought. What was the matter with her – waving and yelling at him like that. She didn't have to come down to the gym and make a fool of herself and him too. He dribbled across the floor and shot. The ball went through the basket without touching the rim.

"Ooh!" Sandy squealed with delight. "Look at that!"

CHAPTER 4

CUTEST FELLOW IN SCHOOL

On Monday morning when DeeDee went into the school building, arms loaded with books, Sandy was waiting for her.

"Hi," Sandy said. "I was afraid you were sick or something and weren't coming to school this morning."

"The bus was late."

They started up the corridor to their lockers. Sandy talked breathlessly about several things until they reached her locker.

"Why don't you go and put your things away," she suggested, "and meet me back here."

When DeeDee returned a minute or so later, Sandy was waiting for her.

"Did–did Doug come to school this morning?" she asked, striving hard to sound casual and only mildly interested.

"Oh, sure. He always does."

"I–I didn't see him," Sandy continued.

DeeDee shrugged indifferently. "I didn't see him either, but he's around someplace."

Sandy waited until they were away from the other kids in the hall. "I think you're the luckiest girl in school," she said.

"Me?" DeeDee's eyes crinkled quizzically. "What makes you say that?"

"Having a brother like Doug. I think he's the cutest fellow in school."

DeeDee almost dropped her books. "Doug, cute?" She turned to stare at her friend. "You must be kidding. You've got to be!"

Sandy sighed. "Oh, no, I'm not. I think he's sharp. And the way he plays basketball!" That wistful tone came back to her voice.

There were some cute boys in school, DeeDee had noticed. She would be able to understand if Sandy had been talking about one of them. But she hadn't been! She had been talking about Doug! DeeDee shook her head in bewilderment.

"When I see him in the hall or on the basketball floor, I just–" Words failed Sandy. She touched DeeDee's arm. "Do something for me, will you, DeeDee?" she asked.

"Sure, anything." DeeDee spoke fervently. There wasn't anything she wouldn't do for Sandy if she could. It would show her how much she liked her as a friend.

"This may sound silly to you, but I–I'm just dying to get acquainted with Doug."

"Oh," DeeDee exclaimed. Her spirits fell.

"You said you'd help me," Sandy said defensively, disappointment lacing her voice.

"Only I didn't know it had anything to do with Doug."

Her friend drew herself up indignantly. "Well," she retorted, "if you don't want to, I guess I can manage some other way."

Then DeeDee realized how her reluctance must have sounded to Sandy. "It isn't that I don't want to," she said quickly, "or that I wouldn't do it if I could. Honest, Sandy. It's not that at all."

"Then what is it?"

"You don't know Doug. He can be so contrary and disagreeable when he wants to be that I–I could scream. If he knows I want him to do something, the chances are he'll do just the opposite for spite."

Sandy sighed that same breathless, wistful sigh that she used whenever Doug's name was mentioned.

"I know Doug has a mind of his own," she said. "I think that is one of the things I like about him. He–he's so forceful."

DeeDee snorted. "You can call it being forceful if you want to, but that's not the way I see it. That brother of mine is just plain stubborn."

Sandy took another breath. "The trouble with you, DeeDee," she said, "is that you're much too close to him. You haven't had a chance to see and get acquainted with the real Doug!"

Someone came up just then and Sandy turned away. "I'll see you later, DeeDee." Her smile was warm and intimate. "You remember what we were just talking about. I want to talk with you about it again sometime."

* * *

With the basketball season taking every afternoon for Doug, Del Davis was alone much of the time. But, since Uncle Clarence Roper had sent their saddle horses up to them from his ranch in Texas, he always had something to do. He would ride home on the school bus, get his chores done and saddle his horse for a brisk trot along the lake or up the road.

Before Doug became so interested in basketball, they had done everything together. Del hadn't had to be alone so much.

It wasn't much fun being alone either, he reasoned as he jogged along the road. He was just about as lonely as that saucy young crow sitting on the fence post on the other side of the road.

At first the incongruity of what he had seen did not register with him. After all, there were a lot of crows around Fairview from early spring until just before winter set in. But a crow on the farm in the wintertime! He became aware of the paradox and reined in.

The instant the horse stopped, the bird took flight noisily. Del stared at him. A crow? This time of year? It wasn't possible. Crows migrated south when the weather got cold. The bird winged higher and wheeled on the chill upper currents, as though on a dismal lonely search for food.

Del didn't know why the crafty bird hadn't gone south with the others of his kind when the leaves turned color and fell to the ground, and the nights chilled. Perhaps he had been too sick or hurt to fly with the others when they left and had been forced to stay behind. How the bird had been able to stay alive in the bitter cold, he didn't know, but his heart went out to him.

When he got back to the house that evening, he talked with Danny about the crow he had seen.

"How do you suppose he has been able to keep from freezing to death?" the boy asked.

Danny shook his head. "I'm sure I don't know, but he could have found a warm place to stay." He paused thoughtfully. "In fact, I'm sure he's found a warm place to stay or he wouldn't have lived this long."

"But would he be able to find enough to eat?"

"A crow is a resourceful bird," Danny went on, "and just about as smart as they come. If there's any food around, he'll find it."

Still Del wasn't satisfied. "I think I'll put a little grain out for him."

Danny leaned back in his chair. "Did I ever tell you about the crow I used to have when I was about your age?"

Del shook his head. "Nope, not that I remember."

"You'd have remembered it if I'd told you," Danny said. "But I don't see how I missed that; it's one of my best stories."

The boy scooted his chair closer to Danny's. "What happened?" he asked. "How did you get a crow?"

"Actually, it was no trick getting him. He got himself caught in a trap somebody had set for squirrels. If Dad and I hadn't come along, he'd have died there. As it was, we had to take his leg off. We had quite a time nursing him back to health."

Danny went on to tell how he had cared for the injured crow and tamed him until he wouldn't leave the place when he was well.

"I asked Dad if it was true that a crow could be taught to speak," Danny went on, "if it had its tongue split. Dad said he didn't think splitting the tongue would have anything to do with whether a crow could be taught to talk or not. And besides, it was too cruel. We decided to see if we could teach him to say anything without splitting his tongue."

Del leaned forward. "Did he learn to say any words?" he asked.

Danny laughed. "I'll say he did. We taught him

the first few words by repeating them over and over again, but it wasn't long until he was picking up words and phrases he heard us use in talking to each other."

Danny continued to tell the boy about the crow he had for a pet and some of the problems Blackie caused, but Del was scarcely listening. He was thinking about the crow he had seen that afternoon. Maybe he just might be able to catch him.

* * *

Sandy Cole had lunch with DeeDee and outlined her plan for getting acquainted with Doug. She seemed confident that it would succeed; in her way of looking at it there was no possible chance of failure. But DeeDee was just as sure that it wouldn't work.

"You can't imagine what Doug's like, Sandy," she tried to explain. "He's simply not interested in girls. It doesn't make any difference who the girls are either. He couldn't care less whether he ever got to know one."

The other girl's eyes gleamed. "That's the kind of boys I find so fascinating. It's a challenge, DeeDee, to get them interested." She smiled confidently. "Doug doesn't act interested in girls now, but he will be."

DeeDee thought about that. For Sandy's sake she hoped it would be true, but she couldn't imagine Doug ever talking to a girl – even a beautiful, well-dressed girl like Sandy Cole.

"Do we *have* to try tonight, Sandy?" she asked.

"It's the only chance we'll have in I don't know how long," Sandy said. "There isn't any basketball practice tonight because of the teachers' meeting, so it's the perfect time."

"There's something else that we haven't thought about," DeeDee said almost hopefully, as though the project would have to be called off.

"What's that?" Sandy asked icily.

"We have to ride home on the bus. We won't have enough time to go down to the Malt Shop first."

Sandy frowned. "I can have Mother take you home," she said.

"But what will you tell her that won't make her ask a lot of questions?" DeeDee asked. "We always go home on the bus."

"I'll tell her you missed it tonight."

Disapproval gleamed in DeeDee's eyes. "But that wouldn't be true."

Sandy stared at her incredulously, as though she couldn't understand why it would make any difference if she told something that wasn't true.

"Yes, it will," she said. "If we go down for a malt and the bus leaves without you, you'll have missed it, won't you?"

DeeDee knew what was wrong with that sort of reasoning, but she couldn't say anything about it to Sandy.

As soon as classes were out for the afternoon

DeeDee stationed herself just outside the door where Doug would be sure to pass on his way to his locker. In a moment he came charging by.

"Doug!" she called out breathlessly. "Doug!"

He stopped and turned back impatiently. "What do you want?" he demanded.

Her cheeks flushed. "I–I just want to–to–" In spite of herself and the fact that she was only talking with her brother, she stammered.

"Make it snappy. I'm in a hurry."

"I–I was just wondering what you were going to be doing for a little while."

"If you don't keep me standing here gabbing all day, I'm going to catch Larry Larson and go home with him to get in some basketball practice on our own." His eyes gleamed curiously. "Why?"

DeeDee was having trouble putting her request into words. She knew what he was thinking, and that made it all the harder.

"OK." Disgust filled his voice. "Hurry it up, DeeDee. Won't you? Larry's going to be halfway home if I don't get a move on."

"No, he won't," she protested. "I just saw Larry going to his locker."

"Sure, and as soon as he gets his coat, he'll be going home." He stared at his sister. "For cryin' out loud, DeeDee. Say what you're going to say so I can get goin'! I haven't got all night!"

"I–I was wondering if–if you'd like to go down to

the Malt Shop with Sandy Cole and me – and have a malt or something."

Suspicion thickened his voice. "OK. Out with it! What's the pitch?"

"What do you mean?" she bristled. "Can't I ask you to have a malt with me without your thinking there's some angle to it?"

"You've never done anything like that before," he said. "It's enough to make anyone suspicious."

By this time, she was desperate. "It wouldn't hurt you any to–to go out with us, Doug," she said, "just this once!"

"Give me one good reason why I should," he countered. "Just one reason."

"Sandy Cole wants to get acquainted with you. That's why."

Doug's eyes widened and his lower jaw sagged in amazement. "What?" He couldn't believe that he had heard her correctly.

"She just wants to get better acquainted with you. That's all."

He stared at his sister incredulously. "Sandy?" he echoed. "Sandy Cole wants to get better acquainted with me? And that's a good reason for missing practice with Larry to go to the Malt Shop with you. DeeDee, you must be out of your mind!"

With that he stormed away, leaving her standing there alone.

She watched him stride down the corridor and

turn to go out of sight. She knew something like this would happen; she just knew it would turn out this way. Now Sandy Cole wouldn't want to have anything more to do with her. She had lost her as a friend. And all because of Doug! If she hadn't been in the schoolhouse, she was sure she would have cried.

Sandy was waiting for DeeDee near her locker to find out what Doug had said.

"Well?" The question flamed hopefully in her eyes as DeeDee approached. "Did you get to talk to Doug?"

"I talked with him." Her disappointment was keen. "I tried as hard as I could, Sandy, but it didn't work. He wouldn't go with us."

Sandy, however, didn't seem overly concerned. "He probably had something else to do," she said. "He is so masculine and strong-willed about everything he does that a girl just can't help admiring him!"

CHAPTER 5

INDIAN FRIEND

The following morning when Doug went to school Sandy was standing in the corridor not far from his locker. At first, he thought she had deliberately planted herself there, and he was furious. He would show her that no girl was going to get her hooks into him. That was one thing for sure. But, as he approached, Sandy began to fumble with her books as though the load was so heavy, she was about to drop them.

"Here," he exclaimed, hurrying over to her. "Let me help you. It looks as though you've got problems." The instant he spoke to her, he was sorry he had, and wanted to turn and run away. But it was too late. Those baby-blue eyes focused helplessly on him.

"I don't know what I'd have done if you hadn't come along just when you did, Doug." There was music in her voice. "I'd probably have scattered my books all over the corridor."

He thrust the books back at her clumsily, for he was confused and embarrassed, and started to move away.

"I do want to thank you, Doug. That was so–so gentlemanly of you."

"That's all right." The color stole upward to stain his cheeks. He was trying to inch away.

"And I–I want to tell you that you played an absolutely fabulous game last Friday. We were all so excited." There seemed to be something wrong with her eyes, he thought. She kept blinking them at him as though she had a piece of sand as big as a baseball in them. "All the girls in Pep Club are talking about how terrific you play basketball and how–how cute you are and everything."

There it was again. He had to be careful around a girl like her because there was no knowing what she was going to do.

"I–I've got to be going," he said, starting to back away again. But he had chosen the wrong direction to get away from her. She was going the same way. Or at least she acted like it.

"Who do you think is going to win Friday?" she asked.

He shook his head. "I can answer that a lot better after the game."

"Oh, we'll win," she said confidently. Her eyes

started fluttering again. "I just know we will with you out there playing your heart out for us."

Doug sighed heavily. There had to be a way out of this. He had to figure out something so he could get away. At that moment he saw Larry Larson approaching. That was his chance.

"I'm sorry, Sandy, but there's Larry. I've got to see him." He turned and hurried away before she could ask him something else and hold him there.

A slow smile came to Sandy's mouth as Doug and Larry disappeared around the corner together. Doug wasn't interested in her yet. She went into her homeroom and sat down, a confident smile playing on her lips. But before she finished with him, he would be. He would be!

* * *

Doug managed to stay away from Sandy for the rest of the week. Once or twice, he saw her coming in his direction, but fortunately he spotted her far enough away to give him a chance to make his escape.

On Saturday morning he planned to go back to town to practice basketball at Larry's as he usually did, but he didn't want to go alone. At the breakfast table he asked Del to go with him.

"We're just going to be dribbling and handling the ball and things like that," he said. "You'd have a lot of fun."

His brother shook his head. "Nope." His lips curled about the word. "I've got things to do."

Feeling terribly sorry for himself, Del got up as soon as breakfast was over and made his way to the barn. It was a bit cold for a ride, but he hadn't seen Jumper for a week or more and was getting concerned about him. It seemed that there were always poachers in the area. One of them just might put a bullet in his tame deer.

Del started down the road, but at the end of the lane he changed his mind. There had been some new snow and the cars had packed it until it was hard and almost as slick as ice. He turned his mount and rode back to the lake. Along the beach the wind had blown the new snow away, making a fairly solid surface for his horse. The wind was even colder than Del had thought it was when he left the farmyard, and he pulled his heavy coat up about his ears. His horse hadn't been ridden for a week and was fiddle-footing impatiently, eager to stretch out in a gallop, but Del held him in.

He hadn't planned on going more than half a mile or so, but as he was about to turn, he saw a thin wisp of smoke spiraling upward from the far end of the lake.

Del spoke aloud to his horse, as he often did when he was riding alone.

"Say, it looks as though somebody's living over there. Let's go and have a look."

He let the saddle horse have his head, and he broke into a fast, distance-eating trot. As he rode, Del tried to think of the area round the end of the lake. He couldn't recall seeing any evidence that anyone had ever lived there before. Actually, he couldn't even remember any cabins over there, but there had to be one at least. Nobody would be living in a tent this time of year, and a fire like that had to come from somebody's dwelling.

Curious, the boy rode on.

At the far end of the lake, he saw footprints in the snow. They were a little smaller than the footprint of the average man, if he was any judge – only wider. He stared down at them for a moment before going on.

A short time later he saw a little log cabin through the trees. In surprise, he reined up. He hadn't ridden over that way often, but he was sure he would have remembered if he had seen a cabin there. Then he realized that it was new.

Del sat motionless on his wiry saddle horse, trying to decide what to do. The problem was answered for him when the door opened suddenly and a short, thickset individual stepped out.

"Hello."

"Hi." Del felt his heart begin to beat rapidly.

For the space of a minute he stared at the man in the doorway. He looked to be about the same age as Uncle Carl Orlis, only he was shorter, thickset, and very dark. His thin, graying hair was cut short.

The stranger greeted him. "Hello, come on in."

Del did not respond to the invitation at first. He remained motionless in the saddle.

"I–I didn't know anyone lived over here," he said.

"No one did until I moved in. My name's Barney Aubichon." A grin split his broad face. "You're the first visitor I've had."

Although he did not repeat his invitation, Del dismounted and found a small tree to tie his horse to. He approached the log cabin slowly, marveling at the way it was built of straight spruce logs, hewed flat on either side and notched until they lay tightly one atop the other. The cracks were chinked with moss.

Barney noticed that the boy was examining the way he had built his cabin. "You come over sometime," the old Indian said, "and I'll show you how to do it. It's not so hard once you know how."

Del's eyes widened. It would be great to learn how to build a log cabin. He could fix a little place of his own down by the lake if Danny could get permission for him to cut the logs and put up a little place. Then he and Doug could go down there on fishing trips and to spend the night. It would be great sport.

The boy followed Barney Aubichon into the cabin and looked around. There was a bed in one corner, a small wood heater, a table and one chair.

"Here, you can sit here." Barney gave him the chair and pulled a small stool from under the table. "Up in Saskatchewan where I came from, I didn't have to make a stool. I used old fish boxes to sit on. Turn 'em on edge and they're just about high enough for a right good chair."

Del sat with the elderly trapper, eating bannock, a biscuit-like material only thinner, and drinking tea, and listening to his stories of life in the North. He and Barney hit it off right from the first. He didn't know when he had found anyone so interesting. He would probably have missed lunch had it not been for Barney. He glanced out at the sun that was almost straight overhead.

"It's about noon, Del," he said. "You're welcome enough to stay; but if you don't want your folks to worry, I think maybe you ought to be getting back."

Del got his coat. "Thanks, Mr. Aubichon," he said. "Thanks a lot for everything. I've had a great time visiting you this morning."

Barney's smile came back. "Just call me Barney."

Del had truly had a fine time that morning visiting with the old Indian. He had almost forgotten the way he had been feeling toward Doug since his brother had been spending so much time playing basketball. When he got home Kay was setting the table.

"Hurry and wash up, Del," she said. "We're about ready to eat."

DeeDee came in. "Did you find Jumper?" she asked.

"Jumper?" For the moment he had forgotten the purpose of the trip that morning. "Oh – Jumper. No, I didn't see him."

Instantly she was concerned. "You don't suppose somebody shot him, do you?"

Del shook his head. "I don't think so. To tell you the truth, DeeDee, I got sidetracked this morning and didn't get to spend much time looking for him. I'll have to go out this afternoon and see if I can find him."

He was going to tell Danny and the others about Barney Aubichon, but he decided to wait a little while. He wouldn't say anything yet unless they questioned him so he would have to tell them in order to keep from lying. Right now, Barney was his own little secret.

* * *

At school Monday morning Doug was almost trapped again by Sandy. He saw her standing near his locker as he came down the corridor. Fortunately, he spied a couple of fellows he knew and scurried over to them like a frightened rabbit. They wondered why he had joined them so suddenly, but he didn't tell them.

Fifteen minutes later when Larry Larson came along, he still had his coat on.

"What's the deal, Doug?" Larry wanted to know. "Did you just get here, or are you goin' home?"

"I didn't just get here," he informed him, "and I don't figure on going home for a while anyway. To tell you the truth, I've been waitin' to put my stuff in my locker."

His friend eyed him curiously. "That shouldn't be so hard. What'd you do? Forget your key?"

Doug did not answer him directly.

"You're goin' that way, Larry. Will you take it for me and put it in my locker?"

"Why me? You've got legs."

Doug hesitated. Too late he realized that he should have stayed completely away from the subject. The chances were that Larry would keep hounding him until he told him the whole story.

"Oh, skip it."

"Oh, no you don't," Larry said. "You don't start something like that and then stop without telling me what the score is. Come on, what's the deal?"

Doug swallowed against the lump in his throat.

"Well," he said, "if you won't say anything about it, I'll tell you."

"You can count on me." Larry was grinning. "What's the deal?"

"It's nothing to laugh at," Doug said. "It's that Sandy Cole. She tries to latch onto me every chance she gets. And right now, she's waiting for me down by my locker."

Larry's grin was broad. "Sandy Cole, eh?" He started to laugh. "Sandy Cole. Now, isn't that something?"

"Larry, you promised!" Doug protested quickly. "You can't break a promise."

"Who says I can't? Sandy Cole? That's great! I saw you helping her with her books the other day. Now she waits for you in the hall. Wait'll the guys hear about this!"

Doug squirmed miserably. "Aren't you even going to keep your word?"

"You wouldn't expect me to keep a story like that, now, would you?" Larry teased.

Doug groaned aloud but said no more to Larry. He didn't know whether Larry would say anything to anyone else or if he was just having a little fun himself. But whatever it was, Doug knew he didn't have a chance of changing him.

He knew one thing. He was going to put a stop to it. That was for sure. And he knew just where he was going to start.

That night Doug was ready for DeeDee as soon as he got home from basketball practice. She was in her room studying when he knocked on the door.

"Come in."

He stormed inside and closed the door. "I want to talk to you!"

"Can't it wait?" she asked. "Don't you see that I'm studying?"

"This can't wait," he told her sternly. "And besides, it's only going to take a minute."

Her temper rose to meet the heat in his flaming eyes. "Now what have I done?"

"I don't know what's going on," he said hoarsely,

"but I'm telling you something, DeeDee Davis! You've got to get that friend of yours off my back!"

DeeDee stared at him. "Whatever are you talking about?" she asked.

"Now, don't give me that stuff. You know as well as I do what I'm talking about! That Sandy Cole has been chasing me all over school and I've had an awful time getting rid of her."

"Oh?" DeeDee's eyebrows arched. "You must have a conceited opinion of yourself to think *any* girl would knock herself out to get to talk to you."

"I don't have any kind of an opinion of myself. Only I can't stand it the way Larry Larson's been razzing me. If it doesn't quit, the story's going to get all over school and I'll never be able to live it down!"

"I don't know why it's any concern of mine," his sister countered.

"Don't kid me! I know what's going on! And you'd better tell her to leave me alone. See?"

CHAPTER 6

DOUG'S NEW APPEARANCE

Danny and Kay were becoming increasingly concerned about Doug. It wasn't that he was giving them any real trouble. He still was very much under their control, but they were concerned nevertheless.

The change that was taking place in Doug's life was so subtle, so minute that it was almost impossible for either of them to put a finger on it. At times they were not even sure that it was real – that they weren't imagining it. Yet, when they considered it soberly, they had to admit that it was genuine.

The first place they saw the change was in his Christian life. There was a definite lack of interest and concern about the things of the Lord. He went to services and young people's the same as always, but his attitude was different. He didn't seem to be listening the way he had only a few months before.

And at home Kay noticed that his Bible was touched infrequently, if at all.

"I'm not positive, Danny," she said, "but I am afraid Doug isn't having his daily Bible reading and prayer the way he used to."

The missionary pilot got a glass of milk from the refrigerator.

"I've noticed that he doesn't seem to have the same interest he had a few months ago, if that's what you mean."

"That's part of it. He used to have pride in his personal appearance, but have you noticed his hair and the way he wears his clothes lately?" She shuddered.

"I haven't pressed him too hard on them," Danny said, "because I've been wanting him to make up his mind on his own. Maybe I had better have a talk with him."

"I think it would be a good idea."

Danny planned on waiting until the following week to talk with Doug, but the next evening he had the opportunity to get the boy alone without making a big scene over it. Kay had gone to a women's meeting at church, and Del and DeeDee were in their rooms studying. Danny and Doug were left in the living room alone.

"Doug," Danny said, "I have been wanting to talk with you about the way you've been wearing your hair lately."

The boy eyed him defensively. "Why? What's the matter with it?"

"Don't you think you're wearing it a little long?"

Doug ran his fingers self-consciously through his hair. "I don't think so. All the fellows are wearing it this way, only most of them let it grow a lot longer than this."

"Do you think it's a good Christian testimony?" Danny asked.

Color came up into Doug's cheeks. "I don't think the length of my hair has got anything to do with my testimony one way or the other. I happen to like my hair long so that's the way I wear it."

Danny was slow and deliberate. "As Christians, Doug," he continued, "we've got to have a different set of standards than those of the people around us. We have to act and dress in such a way that those who don't know Christ will want to be Christians because they want to be like we are."

Doug squirmed uncomfortably. "I suppose I can get my hair trimmed a little," he said reluctantly, "if I have to."

"It's not just your hair, Doug," Danny said. "It's your clothes too. Pants like those you have on now, for example. Do you think they are the sort a Christian should be wearing?"

"What's wrong with them?" he demanded defensively.

"They look to me as though they're about four

sizes too small for you. Most of the fellows who wear clothes like that are only interested in calling attention to themselves. In general, I would say that they're a rebellious lot."

"Oh, I don't know. Johnny Larson wears clothes like these all the time and he's a Christian. I've heard you say so yourself."

Danny nodded. "Yes, it's true that Johnny is a Christian and that he dresses this way," Danny admitted. "But there are a few things you want to remember about Johnny. He's only been a Christian for a short time. He hasn't had the advantage of being raised in a Christian home, so he hasn't had any good, sound teaching along that line. Johnny really hasn't had the opportunity to learn how a Christian should dress."

"I don't think it's such a big deal as you're making it, Danny," Doug went on, his irritation showing. "And I happen to think Johnny's doing OK in his Christian life. You ought to hear how he talks to Larry and me about leaving liquor and tobacco alone."

"I'm glad to hear that, Doug," Danny said. "I've felt, too, that Johnny is making good progress. The point is, though, we shouldn't pattern our lives after other Christians. Christ is the One we are to follow. He is our Example; not Johnny Larson or anyone else."

The boy scowled but did not continue to argue with him. This, Danny was thankful for.

"I'd like to have you think these things over and

pray about them, Doug," Danny said. "We'll have another talk one of these days."

That night Doug lay awake in bed for a long while thinking over what Danny had said. Danny and Kay just didn't understand him. That was the trouble. They couldn't understand why a guy would like the kind of clothes he liked, or his hair the way he had it.

And, as far as he was concerned, there was nothing wrong with the way Johnny Larson dressed. And his hair was neat – he didn't care what Danny said.

Doug prayed about the matter as Danny had asked him to do, but he had already made up his mind. He knew what he was going to do, unless they made him do differently.

* * *

Del was spending as much time as possible at Barney Aubichon's cabin. He would saddle his horse as soon as he got home from school and ride over to the log cabin at the end of the lake. Sometimes Barney would be getting wood, or skinning a mink or a couple of muskrats he had trapped. But it didn't make any difference what he was doing. He always had time for his youthful visitor.

Often when Del rode up to the little cabin Barney would be sitting at the table with his Bible on his lap. The first time Del saw it he stared at it curiously.

"Haven't you ever seen a Bible before?" Barney asked gently, tipping it so Del could see it clearly.

"I never saw one like that before."

Barney chuckled as though he had pulled a joke on his young friend.

"That's really not surprising. It's in Cree."

"That writing looks like the kind they find on those old stone tablets in Egypt."

"It's written in Cree syllables," the Indian explained.

"I understand it better than I do English."

"I didn't know you were a Christian," Del blurted. He hadn't intended to say that–the words just popped out. He looked quickly into his friend's eyes.

Barney's seamed face brightened. "You know, Del, when I was your age, I was worshiping the Indian's god."

"Really?"

"That's a fact. The sun dance and the witch doctor controlled my life. But I knew in my heart that they were not the right way, so I started searching. First, I would follow this way for a little while; then I'd go some other way, but all the time I am not satisfied. There was something about those other ways that didn't seem good to me. Then one day a man came by my trapper's cabin and gave me a Bible. As I read it, I knew in my heart that this was the right way. I gave myself over to God's way and I found Jesus Christ to guide me."

Del nodded thoughtfully. He had never talked with

anyone like Barney since he and Doug and DeeDee left Guatemala after their parents were drowned. For an instant, just listening to Barney made him homesick to be back.

The Indian continued to speak slowly, as though it hurt even to think of the things he was talking about.

"Before I became a Christian I used to do many things I shouldn't," he said. "And when you get older you will be tempted to do some of those same things. But I can tell you, Del, they don't bring any happiness. You want to follow the way of Christ, if you want to be happy." He took a deep breath. "This I have found."

After that Barney made a point of having Bible reading and prayer at some time during almost every visit Del made to his cabin. The boy would sit across from him, his cap on the table, and read from the English Bible while Barney followed along in Cree. Then they would have prayer together.

* * *

Doug did not say any more to DeeDee about her friend, Sandy Cole, but he was careful to avoid Sandy in school or out. If she came down the corridor he turned and fled to the nearest room, or became actively involved in whatever happened to be going on next to him. Once or twice, he found himself talking to a couple of girls who happened to be nearby. That shook him up almost as much as having Sandy nail him in the corridor and talk to him.

DeeDee was still angry with her brother. It wouldn't hurt Doug to be nice to Sandy, she reasoned. He didn't know how a girl felt when she liked a boy and he treated her the way Doug was treating Sandy. But she knew it wouldn't do any good for her to talk to him. That would only make matters worse.

In spite of the fact that Doug avoided Sandy as though she had some contagious disease, she continued to be a good friend to DeeDee, who was grateful that Sandy didn't hold Doug's actions against her. Sandy continued to eat lunch with her and to ask her to the Cole home whenever she could. Mrs. Cole seemed happy to have DeeDee come to visit and did everything she could to make her feel welcome.

* * *

Several times when Sandy was out of the room, Mrs. Cole told DeeDee how glad she was to have Sandy running around with her.

"Her dad and I have felt that Sandy should be allowed to make her own friends," she explained, "but we do get concerned about some of the kids she chooses." There was a brief silence. "Frankly, DeeDee, you're the kind of girl we would like Sandy to be."

DeeDee was embarrassed and didn't know what to say. She certainly wasn't any model that would make anyone want to shape her life like hers. She didn't have really nice clothes, or much spending money or anything.

DeeDee didn't see much of Mr. Cole in spite of the fact that she was spending more and more time at Sandy's. Occasionally he was home for dinner when she was there, but he usually had to go somewhere afterward. Once or twice, he was all dressed up and left without telling any of them good-bye. DeeDee noticed that Mrs. Cole looked sad after that, as though she were about to cry. Even Sandy was more quiet than usual for a time. But nobody said anything and DeeDee soon forgot about it.

She didn't know why she mentioned the place where Uncle Clarence and Aunt Carmen lived, except that she was standing in the middle of the living room floor surveying the beauty of the Cole home, as she did practically every time she visited Sandy.

"You know," she said suddenly, "my aunt and uncle in Texas have a house something like this."

"They do?" Sandy echoed. Instantly she was interested. "You didn't tell me about them before."

"I guess I just didn't think about it." She swept across the room and looked out the picture window. "Their house isn't quite as big as yours, but it is awfully nice."

Sandy dropped to a footstool and pulled her knees up under her chin. "Tell me about it," she said. "Where do they live?"

DeeDee told her about the Circle R Ranch with all the cattle and saddle horses, and how they had several big cars and took long trips whenever they felt like it. She went into more detail than she planned on. It was fun talking about her aunt and uncle and having Sandy listen excitedly. When she finished her best friend was curious.

"Tell me something, DeeDee," she said. "How come you aren't living with them instead of with Mr. and Mrs. Orlis?"

DeeDee was silent for a time. She wasn't ashamed of Danny and Kay. She was proud of them. But how could she explain the reason she and her brothers didn't live in Texas to a non-Christian? How could she tell Sandy it was because her cousin, Phil, accepted Christ and Uncle Clarence blamed her and Doug and Del for it and refused to let them stay in his home anymore? Sandy would never understand anything like that.

"It would be nice," she said wistfully.

"I think it would be super! Imagine living on a real cattle ranch and with people who have a nice big home." She paused significantly. "Then you would be able to have all the clothes and spending money you wanted and everything."

Before DeeDee left Sandy's that afternoon she began to wonder if she and the boys had been shortchanged by having to live with Danny and Kay. After all, the way it was she couldn't have any of the nice things that Sandy had. If she had been able to stay with Aunt Carmen, she could have had everything she wanted. It was enough to make her feel as though they had made the wrong choice in coming to Fairview to live with Danny and Kay.

* * *

Kay began to notice that Del was not staying around home nearly as much as he had been. He was slipping away two or three times a week and was usually gone for several hours. She began to wonder about it and talked it over with Danny.

"He's always been so open and aboveboard about everything," she said, "that this secretive attitude seems all the more unusual. I've never known him to be secretive before."

Danny grinned. "Maybe he's got a girl," he said.

Kay shook her head. "It isn't anything like that, I'm sure."

Danny leaned back and crossed his legs. "I don't know what's going on," he said, "but I'm sure that Del isn't doing anything he shouldn't."

"Maybe not," Kay said, "but I still think you ought to have a talk with him."

"OK. As soon as he comes in, I'll see what this is all about."

Del was late for dinner again that evening. He came in, rubbing his hands, his face white with cold.

"It's getting colder all the time," he said. "I sure hope Blackie is all right tonight."

"Blackie? Who's that?" Danny asked.

"Didn't I tell you? That's what I've named my pet crow – after the crow you used to have."

"I didn't know you had a pet crow."

Del smiled sheepishly. "Well, I don't really have a pet crow. I mean I haven't caught him yet or anything like that, but I've been feeding him until I've got him coming into the yard to eat." Del paused. "You know, he almost knows when I'm going to put out some grain for him. He's usually close by, waiting for me."

Del pulled out a chair and sat down. Ordinarily Danny would have waited to get him alone before talking with him, but in this case he was sure there was a simple explanation that would not be embarrassing to either of them.

"Del," he began, "Kay tells me that you've been making a lot of mysterious trips lately."

DeeDee and Doug both looked up, curiosity glinting in their eyes.

"I don't think I've been making so many mysterious trips," he answered.

"You don't mind talking about it in front of everyone, do you?"

"I–I guess not." Del glanced at Doug. In spite of himself, jealousy crept in. His brother was going to have to remember that Barney was his special friend.

He wouldn't mind sharing him with Doug, but his brother was going to have to realize that he couldn't take over the way he usually did.

"I thought maybe you'd found a girl," Danny continued, "but Kay doesn't seem to think so."

"A girl?" He wrinkled his nose distastefully. "It's not *me* the girls like. It's Doug!"

His basketball-playing brother blushed furiously.

Del went on, telling Danny about seeing smoke at the far end of the lake and riding over to investigate. He told how he met Barney Aubichon and got to be good friends with him.

"He's a Cree Indian and he built this cabin on some land a relative of his owns. He's living there alone, fishing and trapping."

Danny tugged at his ear lobe. This was different than anything he had suspected. He thought Del was taming a new animal or something of the sort.

"I didn't even know there was a house over that way," the missionary pilot went on. "It must not be very big."

"It's not," Del said. "It's just big enough for Barney and his dog and me. But you didn't miss seeing it, Danny. He's only been there a few weeks."

He told them about the new cabin and how the Indian had felled the logs, hewed the sides flat and fit them together to make the little building.

"You've really got me curious, Del," Danny said.

"I'd like to ride over there with you sometime and meet him."

Del brightened. "That'd be great, Danny. You'd like Barney, I know you would. He's a swell Christian and he knows everything about the woods and animals and birds and–" He paused. "Barney's the greatest!"

CHAPTER 7

DEEDEE'S ADMIRER

Although Danny wanted to go to the elderly Indian's cabin the next afternoon, he was unable to because he had to make an emergency trip north to fly one of the missionaries to the hospital. Then a storm swooped in, and he was weathered in at a remote station for a week.

On Saturday, however, he and Del saddled horses and rode along the lake to the Indian's cabin.

"Did you tell Barney that I was going to come with you to see him?" Danny asked his youthful companion.

Del shook his head. "No, but that won't make any difference to Barney. He likes to have company."

The Indian man was not at home when they first got there, but before they had time to dismount, he came hurrying up.

"I saw you coming, but I had to finish setting a trap. I was afraid you'd leave before I got here."

Del introduced him to Danny and the three of them went inside. Danny and Barney got along as well as the old Indian and Del had. He told the missionary pilot how he happened to come down to Fairview. His home actually was in Saskatchewan, he said, but he had come to the States to live with his son after his wife died. When the Indian's son contracted tuberculosis and had to go to a sanatorium, Barney came out to the lake and built the small cabin.

"There's not as much game around here as there is where I used to live," Barney said, "but I can do enough trapping to get the food and clothes I need."

"We're certainly glad to have you as a neighbor, Barney," Danny told him.

The Indian man eyed him intently, as though wanting to be sure whether Danny meant what he said or not.

Danny's smile was friendly.

"Mrs. Orlis and I would like to have you come over for dinner tomorrow," he said.

Barney hesitated, but only for a moment. "Well, I–I think I would like that."

At the door Danny turned back. "There's something else I almost forgot. Would you like to go to church with us?"

Barney brightened noticeably. Then the lights in his eyes died.

"I–I don't know whether I can or not."

"We'd be glad to stop for you."

"It isn't that. I–I don't have the right clothes to go to a church in town."

"You don't have to worry about that, Barney. You can wear whatever you have and the people will be glad you came to worship with us."

The Indian man thanked him. Before Danny and Del left, their host picked up his Cree Bible and held it thoughtfully.

"You know, when I had to come over here and build a cabin, I was concerned that I wouldn't have any friends. God not only gave me some friends, but He gave me Christian friends."

Danny thought he saw tears in the older man's eyes.

* * *

DeeDee and Sandy were sitting together in the lunchroom at school, as they usually did for their noon meal, when the subject of Wally Crowder came up.

"You know Wally, don't you?"

DeeDee toyed with her fork. She hated to admit it, but she wasn't at all sure that she remembered him. She'd heard the name in class, but that was about all.

"I think I know who he is," she said.

"Oh, everybody knows who Wally is. He's a wheel here at school."

Sandy acted as though that was information that

ought to interest DeeDee, but she wasn't sure why. Still, if Sandy thought Wally was important, she ought to feel the same way about him.

"What about Wally Crowder?" she asked.

A tantalizing smile played with the corners of Sandy's mouth.

"I really shouldn't tell you this. Wally'd get mad at me if he knew I was blabbing to you, but he was talking about you the other day."

"He was?"

DeeDee had never talked to Wally that she could remember and would have had a difficult time in describing him if someone asked her to. Still, the information Sandy brought her about him was exciting.

"He thinks you're cute," Sandy announced.

DeeDee dimpled. It was something to know that a boy thought she was nice – especially one of the school leaders. But she knew it wasn't because of herself alone. It was because she had Sandy as a friend that they had begun to notice her. The other kids hadn't even known she existed until she started to run with Sandy Cole. And now she was beginning to be somebody at school too. She liked the feeling of importance, the knowledge that the other kids knew she was alive and liked her.

But Sandy wasn't finished.

"And that isn't all," she said. "He asked me something about you."

"What?"

Her friend smiled teasingly.

"I don't know whether I ought to tell you this or not."

DeeDee waited with growing impatience. It must be something good or Sandy wouldn't act that way. But she didn't know why it should be something that would interest her.

"Of course," Sandy went on, "Wally didn't say I shouldn't tell you, so I'm going to." She took a deep breath. "He said that he'd like to go with you sometime."

DeeDee gasped. She would never have guessed that was what Wally had talked with Sandy about.

"No kidding?"

"That's what he said when I was talking to him this morning." Sandy waited for DeeDee to absorb the information she had just given her. She hadn't told the complete truth, but that didn't bother her. It was right that she had been talking to Wally Crowder that morning and that he had said he thought DeeDee was cute, but that was only after considerable prodding on Sandy's part. And she had been the one who said he ought to go with DeeDee. But Wally hadn't said no, she reasoned, so that was almost the same thing.

"He wants to go with me?" DeeDee felt the color rush to her cheeks.

"That's exactly what he said. And I'll tell you something else about Wally Crowder," Sandy went on. "He's one of the boys who could get just about any girl in school. All he'd have to do is ask and any of them would be tickled to go with him."

DeeDee patted her hair self-consciously. She had thought about going with boys from time to time. Every girl thought about dating, getting married and having a home of her own. But until this very moment she hadn't even considered that she might go with someone now – this very winter.

"I–I don't know whether I would be interested in dating or not," she managed, but there was interest in her voice that she could not hide.

DeeDee didn't know what was happening to her. First Sandy Cole, one of the most popular girls in school, had chosen her to be her friend, and now Wally Crowder wanted to go with her. It–it was too exciting to be true. She must be dreaming!

* * *

Del and Doug hadn't had a great deal of time to be together since the basketball season had started. Doug spent the evenings after school practicing with the team. Saturdays he usually went over to spend the day with Larry Larson, practicing maneuvers Johnny was teaching them.

But the Saturday came when the Larsons were going to be gone for the weekend and Doug wasn't able to spend the day with Larry. So Doug and Del went horseback riding together.

"We could ride into town," Doug suggested, "and see if there's somebody in the gym. Sometimes one of the coaches is there. If we're lucky, he might let us in to shoot a few baskets."

Del shrugged indifferently. "I've got something else to do." He might have known Doug would come up with something like that. But it wasn't going to work. He wasn't going in and spend the day shooting baskets. He'd rather work around the farm than that.

Del half expected his brother to ride into town alone, and was surprised when he stayed with him, riding slowly in the snow.

"Where're you going?" Doug asked after they had been in the saddle fifteen or twenty minutes. "Over to Barney's?"

"That's what I've been thinking of doing," Del replied, "if that's OK with you."

"Sure thing. I'd like to see Barney's house."

They rode along the narrow, frozen lake.

"You ought to get to know Barney better, Doug. "He's a great guy."

"He's nice, all right," Doug said, but there was no enthusiasm in his voice. Del could tell that going out to spend a couple of hours with Barney wasn't Doug's idea of an exciting morning. Doug's indifference irritated Del. He could act that way about Barney if he wanted to, but the elderly Cree Indian was about the best friend a guy ever had.

Barney was puttering around the cabin when the

boys rode up. He came to the door, greeted them cheerily, and told them to tie up their horses and come in.

"I've got some bannock on the stove and it's about ready to take off."

Del's eyes lit. "Oh, boy! Fresh bannock!"

"I knew you'd be along sooner or later today," Barney said, chuckling, "and that I'd have to have some fresh bannock for you, so I thought I'd just as well get it made."

Del went over and sat on the bed. "That bannock sounds good, Barney," he said, "but that isn't why I came to see you this morning. I've got something special to talk with you about."

The man sauntered over to the chair and sat down, leaving the stool for Doug.

"What is it this time?" Barney asked.

"You know that crow I've been telling you about?"

"The one that's been hanging around all winter?"

"That's the one."

Barney nodded. "I've seen him a couple of times myself."

"Can you tell me how to trap him without hurting him?" Del asked.

Barney thought about that for a moment.

"What do you figure on doing with him after you get him, Del?"

Briefly Del told him about the crow Danny used to have and how they had taught him to talk.

"So, you want to get a crow so you can teach him to talk, eh?"

"That's right."

Barney took the bannock off the stove and turned the frying pan upside down over a piece of waxed paper to dump it out.

"The first thing you've got to do," the old Indian said, "is to get this crow to feeding in a certain place every day."

"That won't be hard. I've got him coming into the yard to eat now. I think he's lazy. He just waits for me to feed him."

"Well, start feeding him in the crotch of a tree," Barney said. "Nail a board or a can up there to put a little grain in and get him used to eating out of it."

"Then what?"

"Then you come back over here and ask me what to do next." The Indian winked broadly at Doug.

On the way back to the farmhouse, Del turned to his brother.

"Want to help me catch the crow and teach him to talk?" he asked.

Doug shook his head. "I haven't got time to fool around like that. I'm out for basketball. Remember?"

Del felt the ice grow within him. Why did Doug have to keep rubbing it in?

CHAPTER 8

UNWANTED INVITATION

Sandy invited DeeDee to stay all night at her house again on Friday night.

"Daddy's gone for the weekend," Sandy explained, "and Mother thought it would be nice if you could come over to be company for me."

"I'd love to, only–"

Sandy's smile fled. "Only what?"

"I don't know for sure if Kay will let me."

Sandy could scarcely believe that to be possible.

"You mean she tells you what you can do and what you can't?" she echoed. "You mean she might not even let you make up your own mind about a little thing like staying at my house overnight?"

DeeDee stiffened. "It isn't that," she retorted. "Kay might have something for me to do on Saturday, so I have to talk to her before I make any plans of my own. That's all."

Sandy paused. "I'll bet your aunt in Texas wouldn't treat you that way. She wouldn't make you stay home Saturday morning to do *her* work after you've been studying hard all week."

By the time DeeDee got home she was feeling as though she was the most abused person in town. She had never before realized that she was being taken advantage of in so many ways, until Sandy pointed them out. Sandy didn't have to work at home unless she felt like it. She didn't know why Kay insisted that she help with the work.

DeeDee was sure she knew what Kay was going to say before she asked her about staying with her friend for the night. She was so sure that when she finally asked her, she was almost belligerent.

Kay did not reply immediately. She did not have a good reason for not letting DeeDee spend the night with Sandy, and she and Danny had always had a sort of rule of thumb about letting the kids do things unless there was some good reason why they shouldn't. Yet, she felt uneasy about it. She didn't know why.

"May I?" DeeDee repeated.

"You didn't clean your room this week, DeeDee. You know that's got to be done."

"I'll clean it before I go."

"And you were going to help me scrub and wax the kitchen floor so I could finish making your dress."

DeeDee didn't say anything to Kay about the dress. She didn't want to hurt her feelings. But she wished

Kay would go down to the same little shop where Mrs. Cole took Sandy to get her clothes. According to Sandy, all the girls who were anybody in school went there for their clothes. It was a sort of unwritten law, or something.

"I'll come home early enough to get those things done," she said. "I promise."

Kay's smile winked understandingly.

"If you'll do that, I guess it will be all right."

DeeDee leaned over and kissed Kay impulsively. For an instant she was sorry for all the bad things she had been thinking about Kay. Down in her heart she knew that Danny and Kay weren't that way at all. Sandy only thought so because she didn't really know them.

"DeeDee." Kay spoke softly. "You've been over to Sandy's to spend the night several times, but you've never had her over here. The next time you girls want to get together, why don't you ask her to come out here and stay with you?"

DeeDee straightened slowly. "I might do that sometime," she said. But there was no enthusiasm in her voice. How could she ask a girl like Sandy who lived in a mansion, almost, and had everything she wanted, to come and stay with her?

But that wasn't the worst of it. She would just die if Sandy came to stay for the night. Danny would get the Bible and have devotions after dinner. And if he wasn't home, Kay would take over. Sandy's folks didn't even ask the blessing before meals. What would Sandy think if she came and found out how–how *religious* Danny and Kay really were.

Although DeeDee wasn't aware of it, other changes began to creep into her life. The first time she missed having her own personal Bible reading was when she stayed with Sandy for the first time. After that she got too busy or was too tired to read and have prayer every evening. Once in a while her conscience would get to bothering her and she would open her Bible and read a few verses for an evening or two, but it didn't last more than that.

That was the beginning. There was young people's at church. When she and Doug and Del had first been able to go, she looked forward to the meetings eagerly from one week to the next. The parties were still all right, but the regular programs were a bore. She still went because she knew Danny and Kay would kick up a fuss if she didn't, but she actually wasn't there because she wanted to be.

At first, she didn't tell Sandy anything about it, but the time came when her friend asked her to go to the library with her on the night of the young people's meeting.

Sandy wrinkled her nose distastefully. "Sounds dull to me."

"It *is* dull," DeeDee admitted, surprised that she had even dared to put her feelings into words.

Her friend stared at her. "If it's so dull, why bother going?"

"You can say that because you don't know Danny and Kay," she answered. "They won't let me stay home. I've got to go to young people's, church and Sunday school or Danny's got to know the reason why."

Sandy shook her head. "I don't see how you stand it," she murmured sympathetically. "Honestly, I don't."

* * *

DeeDee thought her friend had forgotten all about Doug because she hadn't said anything about him for a week or so. But Sandy surprised DeeDee by asking her to get Doug to eat lunch with her the next noon.

DeeDee stared at her curiously. "Why?" she asked. The other girl's smile was mysterious and fleeting.

"Just get him to eat lunch with you, DeeDee. That's all I want. I don't care what you tell him, or how you do it, as long as he's with you tomorrow noon."

Concern glinted in DeeDee's eyes. "All I can do is try. You know that brother of mine; I can't promise anything."

She had been hopeful that Sandy would forget about Doug. At least that would keep her from being put on the spot all the time. Doug would never do anything she wanted him to, and especially now that Sandy had started chasing him. If he had the slightest suspicion that Sandy was involved, that would be the end of it. She'd have to think of some good reason to get Doug to eat with her – something he wouldn't connect to Sandy Cole.

She had plenty of opportunity to ask him the night before, but she waited. She didn't want to give him too much time to think about it.

The next morning a few minutes before the final bell, she sought him out.

"Doug," she said, lowering her voice, "I've got something I–I want to talk to you about."

"OK, shoot." He glanced over his shoulder as though he half expected Sandy to descend upon them at any moment. "Go ahead – as long as it doesn't have anything to do with that–that Sandy Cole."

DeeDee paused. "There isn't time to talk now."

Doug scowled his displeasure. "For cryin' out loud! If there isn't time enough for us to talk now, why'd you stop me anyway?"

"You don't need to get so shook about it," she retorted peevishly. "I just wanted to know if we could have lunch together so we could talk then."

He squinted suspiciously. "What're you tryin' to do?" he asked. "Set me up for Sandy Cole?"

"I just want to talk to you, that's all. But if you're afraid I'm going to–to set you up for Sandy, as you call it, just forget it. I wanted your advice about something, but you don't have to have lunch with me if you don't want to. I can get along."

"OK." He sighed in resignation. "We'll have lunch

together. But just don't have that Sandy Cole along with you. That's all I've got to say."

DeeDee breathlessly waited the morning away. She knew this wasn't going to work. Doug would see Sandy and be off like a scared rabbit before she would have a chance to get close to him. Then she'd be in for trouble when they got home that night.

But at last noon came and DeeDee and Doug went down to the lunchroom together. He sat across from her and leaned forward intently. By this time, he was convinced that she did, indeed, have something important to talk over with him.

"All right, DeeDee," he began, concern mingling with the last traces of suspicion in his voice. "What is this all about?"

"I wanted to talk with you about Danny and Kay."

"What about them?"

She cleared her throat. "I've been thinking lately about how boring it is to have to go to young people's and Sunday school and church all the time."

He rubbed the side of his nose thoughtfully.

"Don't you enjoy going to church?" he asked her.

"It's not that. I like to go once in a while, but I'd like to make up my own mind too. I don't like the idea of having someone tell me every move to make, do you?"

He picked up a fork and began to twist the handle between his thumb and forefinger. He had been disturbed about the same thing, he had to admit, but he hadn't known that DeeDee felt the same way. It seemed to draw them a little closer together somehow.

"I'd never given too much thought to it," he said, which was only a half-truth, but he did not tell her that. "But, as far as I can see, there's nothing we can do about Danny and Kay as far as church is concerned. We're not going to change them."

DeeDee got so interested in their conversation that she had completely forgotten the purpose of it until Sandy Cole and Wally Crowder came up to where they were sitting.

"Oh, hello, DeeDee," Sandy said, giggling. "I have somebody here who'd like to meet you."

DeeDee colored delicately as Sandy introduced Wally to her.

While this was taking place Doug sat motionless, trying to figure out what to do next. He couldn't get up and leave. He'd only eaten half his lunch and was still hungry enough to devour a couple of extra hamburgers. He wasn't going to let Sandy run him out and starve the rest of the day.

That Sandy! He'd like to wring her neck!

He hoped she wouldn't turn her attention to him until he'd finished eating and was able to get away, but that was too much to hope for.

That stupid Wally Crowder pulled up a chair and sat down beside DeeDee. With that, Doug knew what was going to happen next and would have retreated, hungry or not, but there wasn't time. Sandy went around to his side of the table and sat down beside him, so casually most of the kids in the dining room would have thought he had asked her.

It was bad enough having to endure sitting beside her. Color crept up into his cheeks and he looked furtively about. Larry Larson was sitting two tables away, grinning like a chimp. Doug groaned inwardly. He'd never hear the end of this. That Larry! Just wait until he got something on him!

But at the moment Doug had a more pressing problem than Larry Larson. Sandy looked at him, eyes blinking like the warning lights on a railway crossing and inviting him to sit closer. He pulled away slightly. He would have liked to pull his chair away from that table and out into the hall, but if he did, he realized helplessly, Sandy would follow him. There wasn't *any* way he knew of to get rid of her!

"Daddy says some of the men uptown are already talking about the way you play basketball, Doug." Her soft voice caressed his name, causing him to blush even deeper. "Some of them are saying you're good enough to be playing with the senior high first team right now."

"I–I wouldn't say that," he mumbled.

"That's just because you're so modest," she told him, smiling warmly. "I always have liked modest boys. They–they're so masculine."

He gulped and almost choked on his sandwich.

That wasn't all Sandy wanted to talk with him about, however.

"Are you going to the class party, Doug?" she asked.

"Class party?" His surprise was genuine. "I didn't even know there was a class party."

"We have one big party a year," she explained, "that's different than the other parties we have." She paused significantly. "The girls ask the boys to it."

Doug shuddered. This was worse than he thought!

"They–they do?" He glanced about wildly. Lunch was completely forgotten. Now the only thing that mattered to him was to get away.

"And I'd like to ask you to go with me," Sandy said, dimpling her prettiest.

Doug lifted his gaze to stare at her helplessly. "I–I–"

"Oh, thank you, Doug. I'm so glad you'll go with me." She got quickly to her feet. "I've got to run now. I'll be getting in touch with you later to tell you when and where to pick me up."

CHAPTER 9

SOLVED PROBLEM

That evening as soon as Doug got home from basketball practice, he called DeeDee aside to talk with her. She eyed him uneasily. She had been expecting this ever since Sandy came over to their table in the lunchroom.

"DeeDee," he exclaimed. "You tricked me! You set me up for a pigeon and I was stupid enough to fall for it!"

"It isn't my fault you accepted Sandy's invitation to take her to the class party. Don't talk to me."

A desperate pleading crept into his voice.

"You got me into this, DeeDee. You've got to get me out of it!"

A tantalizing smile lifted the corners of her pretty young mouth.

"That's your problem."

"Please?"

She surveyed him with obvious enjoyment.

"I can give you Sandy's telephone number, if that will help any."

He stared miserably at his sister. What did a guy do to deserve something like this?

Kay and Del came into the living room just then and DeeDee seized the opportunity to retreat to the privacy of her own room. There she stood before the mirror.

Wally Crowder thought she was somebody special. A smile of satisfaction played on her lips. It was strange that she had never noticed Wally before. He was a wheel at school and a real gentleman.

DeeDee hadn't seriously thought about dating yet. It was something she looked forward to in the future, like a high school diploma and going to Bible school. Now she began to think it might be fun to go with a boy – especially a boy like Wally who treated her as though she was just as popular as Sandy was.

* * *

The date of the junior-high party drew closer and closer. Doug tried not to think about it, but that didn't help a bit. Every day that passed brought it nearer. He did his best to avoid Sandy Cole, but she finally waylaid him in the hall a few days before the party was to be held. He saw her coming, but only seconds before she swooped down on him.

"Oh, hi, Doug," she exclaimed, as though she hadn't stalked him over half the school building to find him.

He stopped because he didn't know what else to do.

"Hi," he muttered.

"I've been wondering when I was going to–to get to see you again," she said.

"I–I've been busy."

"I know how busy you've been with basketball and everything." Her smile deepened. "I can hardly wait until time for the party, can you?"

"I–I want to talk to you about that party," he began, his voice crescendoing in desperation. "I don't–"

Before he could continue, Sandy broke in. "I've got to run, but before I go, I thought I'd better tell you that the party starts at 8 o'clock, so why don't you stop by for me about 7:30?"

With that she was gone, smiling and waving gaily at him.

He stared after her, a certain numbness taking hold of him. There was no denying it; she meant business.

Larry Larson came up just then. "Well, if it isn't Lover Boy."

Doug scowled darkly. "Lay off, will you?"

"You can't fool me. I saw you just now. Sweet little Sandy was looking up at you, those big blue eyes blinking like warning signals."

"Cut it, Larry. I'm in trouble."

"You can say that again. Sandy's got her hooks in you, but good."

"I don't know why she had to pick on me," Doug wailed.

"Oh, but you're such a basketball star. And she just adores basketball stars. Or didn't you know?"

Doug groaned aloud.

* * *

The next two or three days, Doug moved through the corridors woodenly, as though he were under some sort of spell. Sandy Cole had tricked him and now he was stuck! There wasn't a thing he could do about it. He had to take her to that party. But if he did, Larry and the other guys would never let him hear the end of it.

As the time for the party grew closer, Doug's panic increased. Finally, in desperation, he got Danny into the study and closed the door behind them. Danny read the consternation on his face.

"Something wrong, Doug?" he asked.

"Not exactly. I mean, not yet. I've just got to talk to you about a problem I've got."

"OK." The missionary pilot sat down at the desk and turned to face Doug. "Now," he said quietly, "what's the trouble?"

It wasn't easy for the boy to find words.

"Well, I've got this problem." He paused and cleared

his throat. With difficulty he was able to continue. "There's this certain person at school who–who has asked me to do something."

Danny waited.

"Well, I–I didn't get a chance to say yes or no and she – I mean, this person sort of got the idea I was going to this par – I mean, this person figured I was going to do what I'd been asked to, and I–I really don't want to do it, Danny, and–"

Danny suppressed a smile. "That doesn't sound too serious to me," he answered. "At least on the basis of what you've told me just now. What's the problem?"

Doug swallowed hard.

"What do I do, Danny?" he blurted.

The missionary pilot rubbed the side of his nose with his forefinger. There were times when he teased the triplets, but not when they came to him with a matter that was bothering them. On those occasions he gave the problem the same seriousness they attached to it.

"We've got to ask ourselves a few questions before we come to a decision, Doug," he said. "The first one is this: Is this thing you've been asked to do against your Christian principles?"

"It's against my principles, all right!" He spoke firmly. "Only not quite in the way you say. I mean, it isn't unchristian or anything like that."

"Would you have to compromise your faith in any

way? Would your doing it be apt to cause someone else to stumble?"

"I don't think so," Doug answered. "I–"

Danny leaned back, smiling reassuringly.

"Then I can't see anything wrong with your doing what this person has asked you to do."

Doug's eyes flashed. "I can see plenty of things wrong with it. Danny, what I need is help on how to get out of it."

"That shouldn't be so difficult. If you don't want to do what you've been asked to, see this person and explain how you feel. That ought to settle it for you."

Doug shook his head. "It's not that easy."

"Why not?" Danny asked.

"You wouldn't have to ask that if you knew Sandy Cole!" He stopped abruptly. It had slipped out! Now Danny would razz him and the rest of the family would find out everything. He'd never be able to live there again. Crimson rushed to his cheeks.

But Danny was not laughing.

"Why don't you start at the beginning, Doug, and tell me exactly what happened."

Doug related how Sandy had gotten him in a corner where he couldn't get away and asked him to go to that stupid party with her. Only it was more like telling him. And that hadn't been the worst of it. She had scooted away before he got the chance to refuse.

When he finished Danny leaned forward thoughtfully.

"When is this party?" he asked.

"In about a week."

"Why don't you let me think about this overnight? We'll talk about it again in the morning."

Doug brightened. "You mean, you'll help me?"

"I'll see what I can do."

"And you won't tell anyone else about it?" Doug asked.

"I won't tell anyone else about it."

The boy smiled his relief. "You've taken a load off my back!"

* * *

The next morning Danny got Doug aside and advised him to call Sandy and tell her flatly that he didn't want to take her to the party, that she hadn't given him a chance to refuse. Doug thanked him, asked him again about keeping the thing quiet, and went to the phone. He started to dial the number, but DeeDee came in before he finished.

"What are you doing?" she asked. "Calling Sandy?"

He scowled at her. "It's none of your business what I'm doing." He returned the phone to its cradle and turned to face his sister. "And I'm warning you right now, just quit messing around in my life. OK? You've caused enough trouble already."

He tried to phone again just before the bus left, but this time he lost his courage and hung up. He didn't have to phone her, he reasoned. He'd write her a letter.

That night when he should have been studying Doug was composing a letter to Sandy.

Dear Sandy,

I find that

He read it over, started to write again, but stopped and crumpled the paper in disgust. He had to make it clear to her that he wasn't going to the party with her – that he wasn't *ever* going anyplace with her.

Dear Sandy,

I

He started a dozen times but couldn't get any farther than that. She was so stupid she might even get ideas from that "Dear Sandy." A girl like her wasn't to be trusted at all. He took another sheet of paper.

Dear Miss Cole,

I don't

But that was not good either.

Suddenly he got an idea. He didn't know why he hadn't thought of it before.

To Whom It May Concern:

Sandy Cole didn't give me a chance to say no when she asked me to go to the party with her. I never said I would and I don't figure on going. So if you know her, maybe you'd better tell her so she can get some other poor guy to take her.

Doug Davis

Doug read the note with considerable satisfaction. This was more like it. It wouldn't give Sandy any ideas about him, that was for sure. And it ought to put a stop to her chasing him. He put the note in an envelope and sealed it. DeeDee was in the living room when he entered.

"Would you give this to Sandy?" he asked.

DeeDee frowned. "She didn't want you to write to her. She asked you to phone."

"I know, but I decided to write to her, OK?"

"She's not going to like it."

"You just give this to her. It'll explain everything."

DeeDee eyed him with suspicion. There was something about his manner that she didn't like. He was too smug; too self-satisfied.

"Maybe you'd better give it to her yourself."

He caught his breath.

"Oh, no. You give it to her. You will do that much for me, won't you?"

The following morning Sandy and DeeDee met in the hall and talked about their studies and the party that was to be held before long. They were about to separate and go to their classes when DeeDee remembered the letter Doug had given her for Sandy.

"It's from Doug?" the Cole girl echoed, her face lighting.

"He gave it to me last night and asked me to see that you got it this morning," DeeDee said, "but I–I don't know what's in it."

Sandy did not reply. She tore open the envelope and read the note. Momentarily her lips trembled, and anger smoked in her blue eyes.

"That stupid brother of yours!" She crumpled the note in a tight little ball. "I'll show him! *I'll show him!*"

CHAPTER 10

SECRET PARTY

During the next few days Wally Crowder was very friendly to DeeDee, much more so than she had expected him to be. He came up to her in the hall on a number of occasions and talked with her about some of the things that were happening at school. And if they chanced to meet in the corridor, as they did once or twice a day, he spoke to her warmly. The other girls began to notice the attention Wally was paying to her and spoke enviously to her about it.

"I don't know why Wally doesn't look my direction," one girl complained. "I've certainly given him opportunity enough."

That made it all the more wonderful. It was like Sandy said, half the girls in the class would give their clothing allowance for six months for a chance to go with Wally.

Sandy kept telling DeeDee that Wally was going to

ask her for a date, but she wasn't exactly sure whether she was ready for that or not. She liked Wally and everything; it wasn't that. And it was exciting to have him so friendly that all the other girls were jealous of her. But to actually go out on a date with him was something else again. It made her feel queasy just to think about it.

Sandy tried to talk her into asking Wally to go to the class party with her, but she could never do that. Not for the first date anyway. She wouldn't dare.

As it turned out she and Sandy went to the class party together and spent most of the time sitting on the sidelines, watching the games. Only a few of the kids had dates, and a lot of the boys weren't even there.

It was the week after the class party that Wally Crowder invited DeeDee to a party he was having.

"It's to be after the basketball game Friday night," he explained. "I sure would like to have you come over – if you can. How about it?"

She hesitated.

"I'd like to come, Wally," she said. "You'll never know how much I'd like to come, but I–I'll have to let you know later."

Disappointment glittered in his eyes.

"Have you got somebody else you'd rather go with?" he asked petulantly.

"Oh, no. It's nothing like that. It's just that I–I'll have to see."

"OK. You can let me know if you're going to be able to make it." He turned abruptly and left.

DeeDee was miserable. She had wanted to accept Wally's invitation right away, but she couldn't without checking at home first. How could she tell someone like Wally Crowder that she would have to ask Danny and Kay if she could go to his party?

DeeDee was still standing there when Sandy Cole came up to her, eyes bright with excitement.

"Did he ask you?" She spoke in a tense whisper.

DeeDee nodded.

"What's the matter?" Sandy asked. "You didn't turn him down, did you?"

There was a brief hesitation.

"Oh, no. I didn't turn him down." Her voice caught.

"It wasn't that at all."

"Then what was it?

"It's just that–that I don't know whether Danny and Kay will let me go or not."

Sandy's eyes grew round. "That again?" she echoed. "Why wouldn't they let you go to a little party at Wally Crowder's? I've never heard of such a thing."

DeeDee hesitated. It wasn't that Danny wouldn't let her go to parties. She was in Pep Club and went to all sorts of things at school. And so did the boys. The only thing that bothered her was that Danny usually insisted on knowing something about the person who was giving the party, who was going to be there, and what they would be doing. She didn't know whether he would approve of Wally's long hair and sweet clothes. She didn't know who was invited to the party either, but she had an idea it would be kids who dressed the same as Wally.

"Why wouldn't they want you to go to Wally's party?" Sandy insisted.

"Well," DeeDee said, trying to choose words that would satisfy Sandy's curiosity without letting her know exactly what she thought. "For one thing, Danny and Kay don't know Wally or anything about him."

Sandy shook off DeeDee's interpretation of their reasoning.

"That's stupid. Everybody in town knows Wally Crowder. His dad is in the bank and everything."

DeeDee nodded. "I know all of that," she said, "and so do you; but I know Danny too. I'm afraid he would want to meet Wally personally so he'd know exactly what he's like."

Sandy's pretty young face twisted into a frown.

"That's easy. We'll tell Wally what the setup is and let him go over and see Danny. He'll do it."

DeeDee groaned inwardly. "That's just it. Danny wouldn't like either his hair or his clothes."

Sandy's eyes flashed. "How narrow can you get?" She did not reply.

"There ought to be a way out of this without too much trouble," Sandy went on. "If he's going to be so lame we'll have to fool him."

DeeDee must have stared at her.

"I'm not going to suggest that you run away or anything like that," she said, laughing her scorn. "But I think I can tell you how to get to that party if you want to go and still not have any trouble with your 'jailer'."

DeeDee waited uneasily. She wasn't sure just what Sandy was going to suggest.

"Danny and Kay wouldn't care if you came to our place, would they?"

DeeDee shook her head. "They've never refused to let me go over to visit you, if that's what you mean. And they certainly don't care if we run around together. They've both been after me to ask you to come and stay at our place."

"Good. Then it's all settled. You can tell Kay you're going to spend the night at my house. Then we can go to the party and they won't need to know a thing about it."

DeeDee cringed inwardly. She realized that what they were doing was actually like lying. She would be staying at Sandy's home all night; that much would be true. But she wouldn't be spending the whole evening there, and the main purpose of staying at Sandy's was so she could go to Wally's party. It simply wasn't honest.

The more she thought about it, however, the more she was able to convince herself that there wouldn't be anything wrong with what Sandy was suggesting. All the rest of the kids in her grade got to do what they wanted to. It wasn't her fault that Danny and Kay were so strict they had to check on everything she wanted to do. When Sandy wanted to go to a party, she just went. She didn't have to ask anyone for permission.

"Well, how about it?" Sandy asked.

"Well–"

DeeDee's friend took that for approval.

"I'll call Kay right away," Sandy said. "I know just what to tell her so she won't suspect a thing."

Sandy went to the phone and called Kay. At first Kay was reluctant to have DeeDee spend that particular Friday evening at her friend's.

"I've been wanting to have you come out and spend the weekend here with DeeDee," she said. "Why don't you visit DeeDee this time, Sandy?"

"I'd like to," Sandy lied, "but Daddy is going to be gone and Mother doesn't like to be alone in the house. You will let her come over and stay with me, won't you?"

"Well, I guess it will be all right this time."

Sandy hung up and turned triumphantly to her companion.

"There, it's all set. You don't have to worry about a thing. You'll be spending Friday night with me so you can tell Wally that you'll go to his party."

DeeDee should have been happy about it. A few moments before she had wanted to attend the party more than anything else in the world. But now much of the fun was gone.

Sandy lied to Kay. Her dad wasn't going to be away. At least if he was, Mrs. Cole hadn't insisted that Sandy spend that weekend at home. The party still sounded like fun, but how could she enjoy herself going to it when all sorts of deceit had gone into making it possible.

She wished now that she had gone to Danny about the party to see if he would let her go, but it was too late for that. If she did, both he and Kay would have known about Sandy's lie and her own efforts to deceive them. She had to go through with it.

* * *

After school, the night of the Crowder party, DeeDee went with Sandy to her house before the basketball game. Her friend stared at the small overnight bag she had with her.

"Is this all you brought?"

DeeDee nodded.

"But didn't you even bring a party dress?"

DeeDee shook her head. "I–I was afraid to. Kay was there and I thought she–she might ask questions."

"You could have told her you were taking it to the cleaners," Sandy said.

"That wouldn't have worked. She does that herself."

Sandy shrugged indifferently.

"I'm glad it's you who has to put up with Danny and Kay Orlis, and not me. But I guess it doesn't matter about the dress. You can wear one of mine."

DeeDee hesitated. She would like that. Ever since she had looked into Sandy's closet she had envied her selection of clothes. But she felt a bit strange about it too. She didn't know why.

"What about your mother?" she asked. "Won't she care?"

Her friend laughed, a strange note of bitterness creeping into her voice.

"Mother has too many things to worry about to care about my clothes. Besides, she won't even know you have on one of my dresses if you don't tell her."

DeeDee thought about that as they left for the basketball game. Kay knew about her clothes. She knew how few things she had, compared to girls like Sandy. The trouble was that Kay didn't seem to care.

DeeDee knew, really, that wasn't true. She knew that Kay was deeply concerned about her clothes. She wanted DeeDee to look as nice as the other girls in school. But at the moment her self-pity was so great she chose to ignore the truth.

If her real mother had lived, she reasoned, things would be different for her. At the thought of her mother, icy fingers of remorse crept over the Davis girl. Mother wouldn't have let her get everything she wanted, by any means. And especially when it came to clothes. She would probably have been just like Kay – concerned that she looked nice, but not permitting her to be extravagant.

And the party! What would Mother say if she were alive and knew that DeeDee was deceiving Kay in order to get to go to a party? Deceit and lying were two things that had hurt her mother the most.

For the moment DeeDee felt as though she could not go through with it. She would have to call Wally and tell him that something had come up to keep her from going.

But then Sandy began to talk about the exciting parties Wally Crowder had and DeeDee found herself wanting to go more than ever. And she was going to be Wally's date. A smile played with the corners of her mouth. He was the son of one of the most prominent men in town. Most of the girls would have been thrilled to go to his party, let alone be his special friend.

And this was all because of Sandy Cole. Nobody else had ever been so nice to her. DeeDee forced thoughts of Kay and her own mother from her mind. There wasn't really anything wrong with her going to the party; she had to have a little fun.

Doug had one of his best nights on the basketball floor of all the season. He was second to Larry Larson in the scoring department and his defensive play was superb. His man didn't make a single basket until well into the third quarter. He had a knack for outjumping even the taller fellows under the basket to take the ball off the boards. It wasn't that he was so much better than the others; he just seemed to try a bit harder.

In spite of the way he played, Sandy Cole did not lead a single yell for him. That bothered DeeDee more than she was willing to admit. Doug was stubborn, it was true. And she ought to know more about that than almost anyone else since he was her brother. He was so stubborn it seemed that they were arguing half the time. But he was the best player on either team. Sandy ought to let him know the school appreciated his play, even if she was mad at him. But DeeDee didn't dare to say anything to her about it – not after all Sandy was doing for her.

Mrs. Cole had gone some place to dinner when the girls got home. She left Sandy a couple of dollars and a note suggesting that they go out for a hamburger.

Sandy frowned. "Mother's gone off someplace again," she said. "It looks as though we've got to open a can of soup or go out and have a pizza."

DeeDee stared at her. "That sounds exciting to me." The truth was that she didn't get to go out to dinner very often. It was something of an occasion.

"It was exciting for me too," Sandy said, her lips curling bitterly, "the first fifty times or so."

The girls had to hurry to get out to eat and still get back in time for the boys to pick them up at eight o'clock. They were just finishing dressing when the doorbell rang.

"It sounds as though the fellows are here," Sandy said.

DeeDee stared breathlessly at herself in the mirror. The color had fled from her cheeks and her lips were trembling slightly. For one wild moment she feared she couldn't go through with it.

"Do–do I look all right?"

Sandy laughed. "Why ask me? Wally's the one you want to impress."

The boys seemed to be almost as embarrassed and as frightened as she was. That gave her a little more confidence. Only Sandy acted as though a date was an everyday occurrence. Her laughter crackled with gaiety and she seemed able to talk with the boys at ease.

Talking to boys had never bothered DeeDee before. After all, she had two brothers and they were always bringing friends home. But this was different, and she found her tongue strangely tied.

Fortunately, it was a short walk to the Crowder home. When they got there Wally's mother greeted them warmly.

"Some of the kids are already in the basement, Wally," she said. "1 thought it best to have them go down."

"Sure thing. There'll probably be another couple or two along in a few minutes."

As they started down the basement steps the sound

of music drifted up to meet them. Sandy turned to their young host.

"Oh, I've been wanting to download that song. It's cool!"

The Crowder recreation room was bigger and more beautifully furnished than most homes DeeDee had seen. The furniture that had been pushed back along the walls was Danish Modern, and the fire in the copper fireplace was crackling merrily. The kids were gathered in the far corner of the room about the MP3 player.

Sandy saw that DeeDee was surveying the room with real appreciation.

"Like it, DeeDee?" she asked.

"Like it?" Her voice trilled. "I love it. I've never seen a room so–so–"

"Awesome?"

DeeDee nodded. That wasn't the word she would have chosen, but it did seem to fit.

"All the kids love to come here. And Wally can use the room almost anytime he wants to, except when his sister or his folks are having a party."

For a time DeeDee was silent. It would be nice to be living with someone who had money enough to have nice things like this – who would fix up a room attractively enough so the other kids would enjoy coming. No wonder Wally was one of the most popular kids in school! Everybody would like to be friends with someone like him.

While DeeDee was standing in the doorway, someone played a different song and several started to dance.

She glanced at her date uncomfortably.

"You didn't tell me it was going to be a dance," she said.

"Most of my parties are dances."

DeeDee stiffened. Sandy knew they were coming to a dance. Why hadn't she told her? Briefly anger glinted in DeeDee's eyes.

Wally, however, didn't notice. He held out his hands to her.

"Come on. Let's dance."

For half a minute or more DeeDee stood motion-less, staring at him. She had never danced in her life and thought she never would. Mother and Dad had always been so opposed to it.

But this was different, she tried to reason. She wouldn't be dancing because she wanted to, but so she wouldn't offend Wally and Sandy. After all, they had been so nice to her. And they didn't think there was anything wrong with dancing in the Crowder basement. If she didn't dance, she would never have a chance to get with this bunch of kids again. They would all be laughing at her.

"Come on," Wally urged.

Miserably she shook her head.

"Why not?" His lips curled petulantly.

A piece of DeeDee's heart died within her. He

had probably never had a girl refuse to dance with him before. She could tell by the way he spoke that he was getting irritated. She took half a step forward uncertainly, but stopped, unable to go on. She didn't care what Wally thought. There was something inside that would not allow her to dance.

"I'm sorry."

"Give me one good reason."

She swallowed the lump that came up in her throat.

"I don't know how." She blurted the words in desperation.

That wasn't the real reason she didn't dance. She realized that, even as she spoke. But it was the truth as far as it went. She couldn't bring herself to tell him she didn't dance because she had convictions as a Christian against it.

"I'll teach you," he offered.

She glanced about.

"In front of all these kids?" she echoed. "I couldn't, Wally. I'd just die."

He thought about that momentarily. She could tell that he didn't like it.

"I could teach you a couple of dances," he urged.

She managed a thin smile. "Not tonight."

When he saw that she would not change her mind, he stopped urging her. His expression softened.

"You don't mind if I dance with someone else, do you?" he asked.

She shook her head. For an instant, a strange

exultation swept through her. Wally did consider her as someone special. If she asked him to, he probably would have sat down beside her and not danced once. That was the sort of thing that could happen when she maintained a consistent Christian testimony.

Even as she thought about her testimony a numbing ache grew within her. She wasn't really maintaining a testimony, she told herself. She was only deceiving herself. If she was maintaining a testimony, she would have told him why she wasn't dancing. She wouldn't have made a lame excuse about not knowing how.

She sat there, trying to smile and look as though she was enjoying herself.

CHAPTER 11

GUILT FEELINGS

Even though DeeDee had not danced and had no intention of doing so, she felt strangely ill at ease. She knew what Danny and Kay would think if they knew where she was at this moment. She knew what her folks would have thought if they had known about the party and the fact that she had gone. She squirmed uncomfortably and was glad when the party was over about eleven o'clock.

Mrs. Cole wasn't home yet when the boys took Sandy and DeeDee to the Cole house.

"Do you suppose something has happened to your mother?" DeeDee asked, concern showing in her voice.

"Happened to her?" Sandy's laugh was brittle. "She probably won't be home until two o'clock."

They went up to Sandy's room to bed. The Cole girl continued to chatter excitedly about the dance and how much fun they had had, but DeeDee scarcely heard her. All she could think about was the way she had deceived Danny and Kay. She would have liked to go home right then and tell them what she had done. But she couldn't do that. If she did, they would expect her to give up Sandy and Wally as friends. And she couldn't do that – not even for Danny and Kay!

It was late and DeeDee was very tired when she and Sandy went to bed, but sleep would not come. There was an ache within her that seemed to grow with each passing minute – an ache she had never known before. She turned over on her side and closed her eyes. But the instant she did so, she could see Danny staring at her. Danny looked angry but Kay, who stood beside him, had tears glistening under her eyelids.

Now that the party was over and she was back at Sandy's, DeeDee wasn't entirely sure why she had gone to the party in the first place. She had never had any desire to go to a party like that before. She hadn't even enjoyed that kind of music particularly. But something seemed to happen to her when she was with Sandy so that she wanted to be with different people and do different things.

If it hadn't been for Sandy, DeeDee knew that Wally would not have looked at her, let alone invited her to his party. And none of those "cool" kids would even have known there was such a person as DeeDee Davis. She couldn't turn her back on them.

Everything would be wonderful if she didn't have to go back home in the morning and face Danny and Kay. That ruined everything, that and the gnawing hurt that kept her from sleeping. If only she had stayed home! Then she wouldn't feel so miserable. She tried to pray, but that was impossible.

That night was one of the worst DeeDee had ever put in, but toward morning she finally dozed fitfully. When Sandy woke up DeeDee was still sleeping. Her friend turned toward her and rose on one elbow.

"DeeDee."

The Davis girl stirred but did not reply.

"DeeDee, are you going to sleep all day?"

She mumbled something or other and closed her eyes once more. Sandy reached over and jabbed her in the shoulder with a stubby forefinger.

"It's almost nine o'clock. Time to get up."

DeeDee shook herself awake and sat up slowly, rubbing at her eyes. Sandy began talking about the party.

"Every time we go to Wally's we have a blast." She put her arms about her knees and pulled them up under her chin. "Aren't you glad you went?"

"I—I guess so," DeeDee replied.

Sandy eyed her narrowly. "You don't sound as though you had much fun." There was hurt in her voice.

"I did." She spoke quickly. She couldn't let Sandy know about the remorse she felt; it would only hurt her friend and she might not get invited again. "I did have a lot of fun. Only I–I've been wondering what I'm going to tell Danny and Kay when I get home."

"You don't have to tell them anything, do you?"

DeeDee flushed. In her own feeling of guilt she spoke out bitterly against Kay.

"You don't know her. She'll be waiting for me in the living room when I get home, and she'll want to know everything that happened from the time we left school until I get home."

In one way that was true. Kay was interested in what she had been doing and she usually enjoyed sitting down with her and talking over the good time she had had. In fact, that was the way it had all started. Sharing the fun with Kay seemed almost as enjoyable as experiencing it. But she did not tell that part of it to her friend, and Sandy was horrified.

"I think that's terrible," she said. "Kay certainly didn't act like that when I've been out there. In fact, she acted so–so sweet about everything that I got the idea she was always that way." Sandy shook her head. "It must be awful to have to give a detailed report of everything you've done."

DeeDee's lower lip trembled slightly and a feeling of guilt came over her.

"Doesn't your mother want to know where you've been and who you've been with?" she asked. "Doesn't she want to know what you've been doing?"

Sandy's eyes glinted and a certain wistfulness crept into her face.

"My mother doesn't care what I do, or who I'm with, and Daddy cares even less. I could be gone for a month and I don't think he'd even miss me."

DeeDee caught the sadness in Sandy's tone. She almost asked about it, but her friend shook off the mood so quickly she wasn't entirely sure she had even seen it.

"But, I'll tell you this much, I wouldn't trade places with you for anything, DeeDee. I don't see how you put up with it."

"We don't have any choice; they're our legal guardians."

Sandy snorted her indignation. "They wouldn't be my guardians very long; I can tell you that much. If I had to give a report every night of where I'd been and what I'd done, I'd go down to Texas and live with my aunt. That's what I'd do."

DeeDee got up and slipped into her housecoat.

"It really isn't as bad as all that," she said. She got angry with Danny and Kay every once in a while because they wouldn't let her do everything she wanted to do, but she couldn't let anyone else talk about them – not even Sandy. Danny and Kay had some different ideas, but they were really great.

The two girls went down the stairs together. Sandy changed the subject abruptly.

"I can tell you something you probably don't

know," she said. "Wally Crowder has really flipped over you."

DeeDee's eyes brightened, but when she spoke she tried to make it sound as though that didn't mean anything to her one way or another.

"Oh, I don't know," she murmured.

"Well, I do. And I know Wally a lot better than you do. I've been to his parties before. I've never seen him act that way around any other girl. Why, if he'd had his way, he wouldn't have talked with anyone else all evening. And when you were talking with one of the other guys, he didn't take his eyes off you. I think he was jealous."

A smile lifted one corner of DeeDee's mouth. She hadn't thought much about it, but she knew Wally had acted as though he enjoyed her company. He joked a lot when they were together, and one of the last things he said was that he wanted to see her again soon.

It meant something to date a guy like Wally. He was one of the sharpest kids in school. He wasn't like some of those dull kids who went to young people's. Nobody cared whether they ever got to go with one of them or not. Going with Wally meant that she would be somebody "special" at school herself. That was the way those things worked.

"I wouldn't be surprised if Wally asked you to go to the drive-in with him next week."

DeeDee's smile faded. Danny and Kay would never let her go to a drive-in theatre with anyone.

Sandy didn't notice her sudden concern.

"He said that all he's waiting for is to get a guy who's got a car to double date with him. Then he's going to be around to see you." Sandy's smile widened. "You don't know how lucky you are!"

DeeDee ate breakfast thoughtfully.

She had heard Danny say more than once that one sin often followed another. Do something that takes you out of fellowship with Christ and the chances were that you'd soon be flooded with temptations to do a lot of other things that were as bad, or worse. It was no wonder the pain in her heart continued to grow.

Although she had planned on spending part of Saturday at the Cole home, she changed her mind and asked Mrs. Cole to take her out to the farm before noon. Sandy made no attempt to hide her disappointment.

"Do you have to leave?" she asked.

"I think I should."

"I thought we could go up town this afternoon and see Wally and some of the kids."

DeeDee paused momentarily. "I'd like to," she said, "but I should get back home. I've got so much work to do around the house that it'll take me most of the afternoon."

Sandy didn't understand having responsibilities at home.

"Every time we're together you say you've got to hurry home because you've got some work to do," she observed irritably. "You don't ever have time to have fun the way other kids do."

DeeDee bristled slightly at the tone in Sandy's voice. She talked as though Danny and Kay were mean and spiteful and just kept her for the work they could get out of her, when that wasn't the way it was at all.

"I have plenty of time to have fun," she countered, "but I have certain jobs to do at home too. And so do Doug and Del. But we don't mind working; we want to help Danny and Kay."

Sandy laughed depreciatingly. "I'm glad you do," she sneered. "And I'm glad you're the one who lives with the Orlises. Me? I couldn't stand it."

Danny was in the house when DeeDee returned.

"I didn't think you were going to be home until the middle of the afternoon," he said.

"I didn't plan on it." She looked over her shoulder uneasily, as though in a hurry to go. "But I thought maybe I should come back and help Kay with the housework so it wouldn't take so long."

Danny leaned back and crossed his legs comfortably.

"That was thoughtful of you, DeeDee," he told her. "I'm sure Kay appreciates it. And I want you to know that I appreciate it too. It's good to see you assuming responsibility. That shows you're beginning to grow up."

She colored delicately. What if Danny knew the truth? What would he say then? It was almost more than she could bear.

At that moment Kay noted the time.

"If we hurry, DeeDee," she said, "we ought to be able to finish by noon. Then we can have the rest of the day to ourselves."

Gratefully the girl went into the dining room and turned on the vacuum cleaner.

It wasn't long until the telephone rang. Kay came to the kitchen door.

"Danny," she said, "would you mind getting it?"

He went into the living room and picked up the phone. As he talked the smile left his face and his mouth narrowed to a thin line. Neither Kay nor DeeDee noticed the change that had come over him, however. He returned the phone to its cradle and went back to the kitchen.

Kay stopped what she was doing. "Who was it?" she asked.

By now DeeDee had turned off the cleaner and followed Kay to the kitchen door.

"Was it for me?" she wanted to know.

Danny did not speak for a moment or two, but he eyed DeeDee quizzically.

"In a way I guess you could say it was for you," he began. His voice was firm, but there was no anger in it. "A Mrs. Crowder called."

DeeDee stared, eyes widening. Her lips trembled and perspiration glistened on her forehead.

"M-Mrs. Crowder?" Her voice broke. "Mrs. James Crowder?"

"That's what she called herself."

DeeDee was beginning to tremble.

"W-what did she want?"

"She wanted to know if a girl by the name of DeeDee Davis lived here."

The girl's cheeks flushed scarlet. "Did she say what she w-w-wanted with me?"

Danny nodded. "She said that some of the school kids – friends of her son, Wally – were there last night at a party and you had left your purse."

For a minute or two a tense silence gripped the trio. The first flush in DeeDee's cheeks faded, leaving her face a pasty, ashen gray. She turned slowly, staring first at Danny Orlis and then at Kay. Then her gaze lowered.

"I–I–" Words failed her.

At last Danny spoke.

"Would you like to tell us about it?"

She looked up miserably.

"Th-there's nothing to tell!" With that she whirled and almost ran to her bedroom, slamming the door.

Danny stared after her. "Well," he said after a time, "this is a new development."

Kay went over and sat down. "I've been afraid something like this was going to happen," she said.

Danny left the house presently and drove out to the airport to get his logbook from the aircraft. Kay was at home alone. She was sitting in the living room trying to study her Sunday school lesson when DeeDee came out of her room, eyes red and swollen.

"Is there something wrong, DeeDee?" Kay asked gently.

"Where's Danny?"

"He should be back in a little while."

"That's all right," she said, "I–I'd rather talk with you."

Kay closed her Bible and put aside her devotional. "Yes?"

DeeDee sat down across from her, fingers working her handkerchief nervously. It was a long while before she was able to speak.

"I suppose you think I'm a terrible person for–for telling you I was going to be at Sandy's and–and going to that party."

Kay shook her head.

"We don't feel that way at all. You're our daughter, DeeDee, and we love you so very much."

DeeDee pulled herself erect. What Kay said was true. They did love her and tried to make her happy. It wasn't their fault that the Coles had so much more of everything. It wasn't their fault that Sandy could have a whole closet full of expensive dresses and shoes and hats, or an MP3 player of her own and a TV and all the other things that made the Cole home so fascinating.

Danny and Kay did love her and the boys and were concerned about them. They saw that they had clothes they didn't have to be ashamed of, a CD player with plenty of good CDs, and radios of their own. They had ice skates and skis, and hay for the saddle horses Uncle Clarence gave them. In fact, DeeDee had to admit, until she started running with Sandy, she hadn't felt that their home lacked anything.

Her gaze met Kay's.

There was something else that disturbed her even more than the material things she wanted so badly. Something she had never realized before. It wasn't alone all the fine things that belonged to Sandy that caused DeeDee trouble. It was the effect her friend had on her own life. When she was with Sandy, she did things she shouldn't do – things she actually didn't want to do. Sandy was having a bad influence on her own Christian life.

"I–I'm awfully sorry," she said at last.

Kay eyed her quizzically. It seemed that there was something more in her simple apology than being sorry she had gone to the party.

"Is there something else you would like to tell me, DeeDee?"

She moistened her lips with the tip of her tongue. Briefly it looked as though she was about to speak, but she did not. Instead, she shook her head.

"I'm glad this matter is out in the open," Kay told her.

"Let's forget it now, shall we?"

DeeDee nodded. "We'll forget that it ever happened."

She put her arms about Kay and kissed her impulsively.

It wasn't going to be easy for her to push aside the influence of Sandy's home and all the wonderful things they had. It wasn't going to be easy for her to push aside Sandy's influence on her life. But she was going to try. With God's help, she was going to try.

THE
DANNY ORLIS
SERIES

The Danny Orlis series, by Bernard Palmer, delivers a blend of adventure, mystery, and suspense through various settings—from the Canadian wilderness to Guatemalan jungles. Danny Orlis, an adept outdoorsman, skilled athlete, and committed Christian, employs his quick thinking, calm bravery, and biblical solutions to confront everyday problems and hair-raising dangers. Early stories focus on Danny navigating school life, sports, and outdoor challenges, while in later books, Danny and his wife Kay provide wisdom and guidance to youngsters facing lifelike situations and challenges. Having sold over two million copies, this series has made Palmer a renowned author in Christian youth literature. Palmer is also the author of the Felicia Cartright series and various other series for Christian youth.

AVAILABLE FROM WWW.ANEKOPRESS.COM